Not One Damsel in Distress

Not One Damsel in Distress

WORLD FOLKTALES FOR STRONG GIRLS

Collected and told by

Jane Yolen

With illustrations by

Susan Guevara

Silver Whistle • Harcourt, Inc.

SAN DIEGO   NEW YORK   LONDON

The author gratefully acknowledges the following for permission to retell from previously
published material: For "Nana Miriam": Steven H. Gale, for permission to retell "Nana Miriam," from
West African Folktales (NTC Publishing, 1995). For "The Pirate Princess": Retelling based on "Pirate
Princess" by Howard Schwartz, from *Elijah's Violin* (Oxford University Press); copyright © 1983 by
Howard Schwartz; reprinted by permission of Howard Schwartz, c/o Ellen Levine Literary Agency, Inc.
For "Brave Woman Counts Coup": From *American Indian Myths and Legends* by Richard Erdoes
and Alfonso Ortiz, editors; copyright © 1984 by Richard Erdoes and Alfonso Ortiz; adapted by
permission of Pantheon Books, a division of Random House, Inc.

Library of Congress Cataloging-in-Publication Data
Yolen, Jane.
Not one damsel in distress: world folktales for strong girls/collected
and told by Jane Yolen; illustrated by Susan Guevara.
p.   cm.
"Silver Whistle."
Includes bibliographical references (pp. 113–116).
Summary: A collection of thirteen traditional tales from various parts of the world,
each of whose main characters is a fearless, strong, heroic, and resourceful woman.
1. Fairy tales.   2. Women—Folklore.   [1. Fairy tales.   2. Women—Folklore   3. Folklore.]
I. Guevara, Susan, ill.   II. Title.
PZ8.Y78At   2000
398.22'082—dc21   99-18509
ISBN 0-15-202047-0

Text set in Aldus
Designed by Lori McThomas Buley

First edition
A C E G H F D B
Printed in the United States of America

Contents

An Open Letter to
My Daughter and Granddaughters

THIS BOOK IS for you. It is for you because I never had this book when I was growing up. I played with my brother, Steve, and my best friend, Diane, in New York City's Central Park; and I was King Arthur or Merlin or Lancelot because I didn't know Bradamante. I was Robin Hood because Maid Marian wasn't a better shot.

This book is for you because for the longest time I didn't know that girls could be heroes, too. Not heroines. Not sheroes (a term Maya Angelou made up). Because *heroines* and *sheroes* sound like lesser or minor heroes, just as *poetess* and *authoress* sound as if they are not as good as their male counterparts.

This book is for you because in it are folktales about heroes—regular sword-wielding, spear-throwing, villain-stomping, rescuing-type heroes who also happen to be female. Stories that range from the medieval armored knight Bradamante to the magic-wielding African Nana Miriam, from the Jewish pirate princess to the serpent-slaying daughter of a samurai, from the Scottish lassie who faces down the queen of the fairies to the American girl who foils an Ozark highwayman.

Hi, Xena!

This book is for you because those stories have always been around, hidden away in the back storeroom of folklore. Disguised. Mutilated. Truncated. Their feet bound as surely as the Chinese bound the feet of young noblewomen even into this century.

This book is for you because the stories were there not only in folk traditions and in folklore waiting to be discovered but in history, as well. For, once upon a *real* time, there were actual young women who, sometimes in full disguise—and sometimes in no disguise at all—went off to do battle.

For example, there were women known as Amazons—goddess-worshiping tribes—in North Africa, Anatolia, and the Black Sea area, and in Greece's ancient Cappadocia, Samothrace, and Lesbos. These were tribes supposedly made up of women warriors who were said to have been the first to tame horses and therefore were invincible in battle. They were known as the founders of cities and sanctuaries.

According to David E. Jones, in *Women Warriors: A History*, the Amazons wore long trousers, midthigh-length coats, leather boots, and Phrygian hats. They carried small crescent-shaped shields, light battle-axes, and short swords. Sometimes they had war spears and bows. One group—called Scythians—would not even let their girls get married until the girls had killed three enemies in battle.

More than a few barbarian armies in the long ago included women warriors and battle queens. In fact, many believed that female magic was necessary for any victory in war. If you look in the Bible, there is the priestess-queen Deborah accompanying the troops into battle to cast victory spells. Or in Arabic texts you can read of Queen Bat Zabbai of Palmyra—now Syria—who hunted with the best of the men and, well armored, led her armies against Egypt. The Romans named her Septima Zenobia. There was also Queen Hind al-Hunud, who is described as "brandishing a broadsword with great gusto" in a seventh-century battle against Muhammad. The ancient texts are full of such tough-minded women.

European annals are also sprinkled with them: Graine or Grace O'Malley, the Irish pirate queen who lived in Queen Elizabeth's day; Queen Maud, who led her army against her usurping cousin in twelfth-century England.

And a fabulous but hidden part of history is the fact that in England in the fourteenth century there were women actually fighting in tournaments alongside the knights. A chronicle of the time states that "when the tournaments were held, in every place a company of ladies appeared in the diverse and marvelous dress of a man, to number sometimes of about forty, sometimes fifty ladies," though it adds rather bitterly, "and in such manner they spent and wasted their riches and injured their bodies with abuses and ludicrous wantonness."

In China lived Asia's most famous woman warrior, the fifth-century Hua Mu-Lan, who replaced her father—too ill to fight—in the emperor's army. And Madame Ching, the nineteenth-century Chinese pirate—surely the greatest pirate the world has ever known—commanded two thousand ships and seventy thousand pirates.

In the Beja tribe in Africa there was a corps of women lancers. And in the 1840s a battalion of spear women protected the king of Behr. The African Yoruba people have a long tradition of female military heroes. In fact, throughout the African continent there are "priestess chiefs" who rule in both war and peace.

Native American tribal histories are full of similar stories: a secret society of Cheyenne women warriors; the famed Crow warrior Woman Chief, who battled the traditional Blackfoot enemy; the Blackfoot girl Brown Weasel, later called Running Eagle, who learned hunting and warfare from her brother—and countless others whose names we may never know because they were not recorded.

I never knew their stories when I was your age. Not in real life. Not in folklore.

But I do now.

THIS BOOK IS for you because I think the tongue is mightier than the sword. As is the pen.

Most of the time.

But this book is for you because it is important to know that anyone *can* be a hero if they have to be. Even girls.

Especially girls.

Especially you.

Your loving

Nana

GREECE

Atalanta the Huntress

Hail Artemis, goddess of the hunt,
patron of young women warriors

THERE WAS A king named Iasus, a cruel, unfeeling man who took his newborn daughter into the Calydonian forest on the far borders of his kingdom. There he put her down on the forest floor saying, "I wished for a boy, and this is what I got. I will not have you."

Then he turned and left.

The child lay under the canopy of leaves and after a while, growing hungry, she began to cry. It was the high wail of an infant who wants only one thing.

A mother bear happened to pass by. Curious about that strange yet familiar cry, she came over and snuffled at the child—great furry head against the smooth one. Unafraid, the child reached up and touched the bear's nose. In return the bear began to lick her with a rough, tickly tongue.

For a moment the child forgot her hunger and cooed with delight. And the bear, charmed by the cooing sound, lay down heavily by the baby's side.

The bear had just weaned her own cubs, but here was a cub of another

1

sort. So without quite understanding the why of it, she offered her milk to the human cub.

The baby drank, slept, woke, cooed, drank again.

And lived.

EVENTUALLY THE BEAR was ready to wean the human cub, but the human cub would not let her go, trotting through the woods after the bear with incredible speed.

And so a year went by, and then a second. In the third year the bear went missing—the child never knew why—and a passing hunter heard the child weeping, picked her up, and brought her home to his childless wife.

"We shall call this little girl Atalanta," the hunter said. "And she will be a blessing to us in this, our old age."

"We will give honor to Artemis, goddess of the hunt," added his wife, "who preserved her in the forest until you could find her."

And so they took Atalanta in and taught her woodcraft and house craft, hunting and cooking. She was as easy in the woods at thirteen as she had been at three: swift, eagle-eyed, and strong.

NOW, WHEN ATALANTA was thirteen, her stepparents died. She went at once to Artemis's shrine in the forest and knelt down. If she had no mother, Artemis would be her mother. If she had no father, Artemis would watch over her.

"Tell me, goddess," she whispered, "what I must do now."

"Disaster will follow the men you meet," came the reply.

"Then I shall stay away from the company of men," said Atalanta.

BUT IT WAS easier to say this than to do it, for the Calydonian forest was home to a great red-eyed boar. That monster had been set down by

Artemis, who was angered that King Oeneus of Calydon had neglected to give her honor.

The boar tore down the grapevines, ate the olives from the trees, trampled the green corn, and slaughtered sheep in their pens. Neither shepherd nor sheepdog nor farmer could stand against the beast. Soon the storehouses of Calydon stood empty and the country-people fled to the safety of the cities.

"What shall we do?" cried the people of Calydon.

"What shall *I* do?" cried the king.

The king's son, Meleager, the fairest prince in twenty kingdoms, who had sailed with the hero Jason on the *Argo* after the Golden Fleece, said, "I will hunt this boar, Father." But though he tried, this mighty spear-thrower, he had no success. So he called his friends to come and help.

The most famous heroes and the most famous hounds came to the chase. They stayed many days getting ready to hunt, spending their nights feasting and drinking red wine, their days boasting about past feats.

ATALANTA CAME, TOO, for the boar had ruined all the paths she had loved in the forest and had torn up the trees under which she had played as a child. Yet, try as she might, she, too, had had no success in tracking the boar and killing it, which was strange since she knew every inch of the woods.

"This is some game of the gods," Atalanta had said to herself. "I will ask the king of Calydon for help."

She marched to Oeneus's palace and mounted the great marble steps that were worn down from the passage of many feet. Her golden hair was pulled tightly back in a knot, and her face looked now like a girl's, now like a boy's. Over her left shoulder she carried an ivory quiver. There was a mighty hunting bow of ash in her left hand.

"I am Atalanta of the woods," she announced. "I need help with a fierce red-eyed boar."

The heroes congregating on the steps ignored her. They continued with their boasting tales, their voices raw and deep from the late-night feasts, the red wine, the telling of tales.

Atalanta said again, "I have come for help. Will no one go with me to hunt this boar?"

"Who is this mere girl who would hunt with heroes?" cried Castor, and his twin, Polydeuces, echoed him, "She cannot be allowed on a hunt."

But, standing to one side, Prince Meleager had been considering the hunters, deciding who was fit. When he saw Atalanta, he remembered hearing stories of a young woman living alone in the forest, and thought, *Happy the husband who wins this girl.* He said, "Welcome to the chase, Atalanta, huntress daughter of Artemis."

SO, THE HUNT in the Calydonian forest began.

Atalanta knew the forest better than all. Therefore it was she who led them to the latest tracks of the great boar. And there some of the heroes set out snares, and some sent off the hounds, but most took up the trail.

At last they came to a great gorge where reeds and swamp grass and osier grew thick and wild. The hounds—gray and black and tan—began to bay at the brush, and the thicket boiled with their short, sharp attacks.

Rushing forward, spears held before them, the heroes made a great half circle around the place. They called out to one another, lending courage with their voices.

"Ho!" cried Castor.

"Here," Polydeuces answered.

"Stand fast," Meleager called.

Only Atalanta was silent, intent on the bending willow, the smooth sedge, the tangled reeds.

Suddenly the boar—his rough knotted neck, bristles like sharp spikes, tusks as big as battle-axes—charged forward from the thicket. His head slashed right, then left, then right again. A storm of blood rained down.

When it was over, three men and three hounds lay dead on the ground, and a fourth—great Nestor—using his spear as a vaulting pole, leaped into the branches of a tree.

Then the boar broke free and fled into another thicket, this one wilder and more impenetrable than the last.

"He has gone to ground," shouted Meleager. "We shall not get him now."

But no sooner had he spoken than the boar—having got a next wind—charged out again, scattering men, dogs, spears.

Only Atalanta stood her ground, aimed her arrow, and let it go. It pierced the red-eyed boar behind the ear, and the great beast, foaming at the mouth, fell to its knees.

At that the heroes rushed forward, each clamoring to deliver the deathblow. Still, the great boar was not done with them. It raised its head and, with its reddened tusks, caught the nearest man—Ancaeus—in the groin, killing him with a single slash. Then another hero tried and was slain. And another. The monster, in its own death throes, looked to slay them all.

At last Meleager stepped up behind the boar and plunged his spear into the great humped back. The spearhead missed bone and hit heart, and finally the monster died. But four more heroes and six more hounds lay dead at its feet.

"They died well," said Castor. And his twin echoed, "Well indeed."

"No death is a good one that comes too early," said Meleager. Then he cut off the boar's tusks with his knife and skinned the beast. He offered these to Atalanta, saying, "Though they are by rights mine who dealt the deathblow, you deserve to share in the honor."

Atalanta took the prizes with a nod of her head.

"Why give the girl what was bought with heroes' blood?" asked Plexippus, Meleager's uncle.

"Yes," his uncle Toxeus added, "you slew the boar with your spear. Keep the hide and tusks yourself, Meleager."

But the prince shook his head. "She is the one who stopped the boar with an arrow. I could not have speared it had she not brought it to its knees."

"A prize to a girl? You lovesick pup!" cried Plexippus.

Toxeus, a man only a bit older than Meleager himself, grabbed up the hide and tusks from Atalanta and held them out.

Furious to be so thwarted, Meleager cried, "You shall know the difference between threat and deed." And before anyone could stop him, he took his sword and thrust it first into the side of Toxeus and then into the heart of Plexippus, killing them both.

Atalanta fell to her knees. "O Artemis!" she cried. "Is this what you meant when you told me that disaster follows the men I meet?" She left the heroes standing there, counting their dead, and ran swiftly into the depths of the woods, alone. She was not to know that fair Meleager would die within days, of a fierce magic, and the house of Calydon would be brought to ruin, for she never went to that side of the forest again.

ATALANTA'S FAME IN the Calydonian hunt and her ability to run finally brought her to the attention of King Iasus, the father who had first left her in the forest. When he heard the story of how she had been brought up first by a bear and then by a huntsman, he realized that she was his abandoned daughter.

With a troop of soldiers, he scoured the forest until he found her. Descending from the litter that carried him, he knelt before her. "I was wrong to have left you, but Artemis watched over you," he said. "Will you forgive this poor old man who has no sons and only now a daughter?" There were tears in his eyes.

She forgave him, for that was in her nature, though by rights she could have hated him.

But no sooner had she gone to live in the palace, feasting on dainty dishes and listening to the serenading of lyre and harp, than her father said, "You must marry, my daughter. You must give this poor old man grandsons."

"Disaster follows the men I meet," Atalanta said, "and so it will be if I wed."

But King Iasus would not be satisfied. "After the virgin Artemis, one must honor Aphrodite, goddess of love, and Hestia, goddess of hearth and home."

Day after day he said the same. At last Atalanta could not stand it any longer. To be left in peace, she declared to her father, "I will marry only a man who can beat me in a footrace."

"Is that all?" asked her father, and he decreed that it be so.

But Atalanta, guided by Artemis, won race after race. No man came even close to winning.

So her father further declared, "Anyone who races and loses will likewise lose his head." In this way, he thought to stop so many rash and unprepared men from challenging Atalanta.

Now, one young prince, Melanion—fairer than the dawn—came to the court of King Iasus. He saw the lovely Atalanta and fell hopelessly in love with her. But he did not want to lose his head, and he knew that he could not outrun her. So he went at once to the temple of Aphrodite, goddess of love, and knelt all night in prayer.

In the morning he found three golden apples by his side and knew that Aphrodite had answered him.

Going to the king, he said, "I am ready for the racing challenge, Your Majesty. I love your daughter."

King Iasus shook his head. "Are you certain, Prince Melanion? For if you do not beat her in the race, you will die."

"I will win," said Melanion. "Aphrodite has told me so."

SO, THE RACE BEGAN.

For the first hundred yards they kept pace, for Atalanta liked this young man with his fair brow and long dark hair.

But then, remembering what Artemis had told her about disaster following the men near her, she started to race away from him.

Melanion took out one of the golden apples and tossed it in front of the speeding girl.

The apple sparkled in the sun. As it rolled, little flickers of sunlight on the apple's skin burst into tiny flames. Atalanta could not take her eyes off the golden fruit. She desired it above all things. Stooping down, she picked it up.

And Melanion passed her by.

Putting the apple into a leather pocket hanging on her belt, Atalanta stood up and began to run. By the second hundred yards she had caught up with Melanion. And then she began to pass him.

He tossed the second golden apple into her path. Again, the sparkle of the rolling apple, igniting sunlight into flames, fascinated her. She desired that second apple above all things. She stopped, stooped, picked it up.

And Melanion was gone on ahead once more.

Atalanta put the second apple in the leather pocket and started running again, this time catching up with Melanion before the third hundred yards were gone.

But just before the finish line, he tossed the third golden apple off to the side. It, too, sparkled and flamed, and Atalanta—not even realizing what she was doing—chased after it.

Melanion crossed the finish line first. Then, turning to Atalanta, he went down on his knees. "I have won the race but would have you wed me for love, not for a promise."

With the three golden apples safe in her pocket, Atalanta smiled at him. "I see that if I do not marry you, more young men will meet disaster because of me. Perhaps that is what Artemis meant." She gave him her hand and raised him up, vowing for the good of her people never to race again.

Then, side by side, they stood before the priests and made their marriage vows. They lived many happy years, always remembering to honor both Artemis and Aphrodite, who had brought them together.

NIGER

Nana Miriam

*In a village where only men are warriors,
the greatest warrior is a young woman*

ONCE, IN A SMALL VILLAGE by the great river Niger, there lived a man named Fara Maka and his daughter, Nana Miriam.

Now, Fara Maka was a tall man, tall as a tree. He had arms as strong as tree limbs. Legs as thick as roots. And he was ugly. Very ugly.

His daughter, Nana Miriam, was tall and strong like her father. But as ugly as he was—she was that beautiful. And smart. Very smart.

Fara Maka was proud of his tall, strong, beautiful, smart daughter, and he taught her all he knew. He taught her the names of things: perch and tiger fish in the river, acacia and doom palm trees and the growing herbs on the land. He taught her the names and the uses of all things.

Nana Miriam learned everything her father taught her, and she learned one thing more, for she had magic powers that no one knew about. But she did not tell anyone of those powers, for it was said by her people, "He who boasts much can do little."

Now, at that time which we are talking about—not now or then but somewhere in between—a great hippopotamus lived in the Niger. But it was no ordinary hippopotamus. It was a monster with an insatiable hunger. And every time the rice crop—the main food of the Songhai people—was ready to be harvested, the monster hippopotamus rose up out of the River Niger, water raining off its gigantic back. It waddled onto the land and devoured the entire crop.

Time after time, season after season, the monster ranged up the river and down, devouring the rice for miles. And at last this caused a famine in the land.

The village warriors went out with their spears, sharpened and ready, to hunt the monster. But they could do nothing against it, for it was a shape-shifter as well. Whenever a spear was thrown at the hippopotamus's broad side, the animal changed—sometimes into a crocodile or a manatee. Once, it even became a two-hundred-pound perch and swam quickly away.

Fara Maka went out to hunt the beast, carrying seven spears. When he found the monster at last, the beast opened its great mouth and roared. There were pots of fire hanging around its gigantic neck.

Fara Maka's knees trembled, but still he threw his spears at the monster, one by one by one. And each time, the spears were destroyed by the pots of fire, bursting into flame like shooting stars.

The monster roared again, as if laughing at Fara Maka, before turning its back and going on to the next field of rice.

What could Fara Maka do? He went to Kara-Digi-Mao-Fosi-Fasi, a member of the neighboring Tomma people, who had a reputation for hunting nearly as great as his own.

"Will you hunt this beast with me?" asked Fara Maka.

Kara-Digi-Mao-Fosi-Fasi agreed. "And I will bring along my one hundred and twenty hunting dogs."

"That is good," said Fara Maka, though the hundred and twenty hunting dogs made him nervous, for each had an iron chain around its neck, and teeth that were pointed, and eyes that shone in the dark.

So, Fara Maka and Kara-Digi-Mao-Fosi-Fasi went out on the trail of the monster with the hundred and twenty hunting dogs. It was not a difficult trail to find, for the giant hippopotamus left a path of destruction wherever it went.

Soon they came upon the monster, and the dogs were turned loose, one by one by one. Their chains rattled as they ran, and they gnashed their pointed teeth, and they bayed at the hippopotamus, who turned lazily to meet them.

The monster saw the dogs and just laughed. "Do you people who live on the Niger not say that 'The rat cannot call the cat to account'?" And with that, one by one by one, the monster hippopotamus grabbed up each dog, turned it around, and swallowed it whole, starting with the tail. When the last dog was devoured, the monster turned its back on Fara Maka and Kara-Digi-Mao-Fosi-Fasi, and waddled back to the rice field, where it consumed the last of the crop.

Fara Maka and Kara-Digi-Mao-Fosi-Fasi ran off in terror, and they ran all the way back to Fara Maka's house. There, trembling, they told Nana Miriam what had happened.

"Well," said Nana Miriam, standing up, "it is time for me to see this monster for myself."

Fara Maka trembled. "Daughter, you are strong and you are wise. But no hunter's spear can touch that thing. No hunter's dog can fight it. Do not go."

Kara-Digi-Mao-Fosi-Fasi agreed. "You are but a female," he said. "Listen to your father. Do we not say, 'Ashes fly back into the face of him who throws them'? This is too dangerous a thing for a mere girl."

But Nana Miriam would not be persuaded. She went forth anyway, a spear in one hand, her juju bag filled with charms in the other.

It was not long before she came upon the monster, who was devouring yet another rice field on the banks of the river.

When the hippopotamus saw her, it stopped eating and turned. It smiled a broad hippopotamus smile, showing strong hippopotamus teeth. "Girl, girl, I know why you are here. You wish to stop me."

"That I do," said Nana Miriam.

"But do you not know that no human being can kill me?" said the hippopotamus. "All the hunters in your village have tried. Your father, Fara Maka, has tried. Even Kara-Digi-Mao-Fosi-Fasi and his one hundred and twenty dogs have tried. What makes you think a mere girl can stop me?"

Nana Miriam put down the spear and held the juju bag up. "We will not know the answer to that until we engage in battle. I am ready if you are, monster."

The monster smiled again, and this time it gave more than a mere hippopotamus smile. "I am ready, girl!" The shout was full of flames, which set the rice field afire. Soon a wall of fire sprang up between the monster and Nana Miriam.

Nana Miriam reached into her juju bag and pulled out a magic powder. She flung the powder onto the fire, and at once the flames turned to water, which rained down upon the field.

"That was too easy, monster," she said.

"Ah!" shouted the hippopotamus. "What will you do with this then, girl?" And at its shout, a wall of iron appeared between them.

Nana Miriam reached back into the juju bag, and this time she took out a small magic hammer that grew and grew into a great magic. One blow, then another—Nana Miriam pounded the hammer against the iron wall. And in a matter of minutes, the wall was broken into small pieces by the force of her blows.

"Do you have something more?" cried Nana Miriam. "Or is that all?"

For the first time, the hippopotamus monster looked nervous. Lines of worry appeared on its broad brow. Perspiration flowed freely down its face.

It turned from Nana Miriam and shifted its shape, becoming a river that flowed swiftly toward the Niger.

But Nana Miriam was ready. Once more she reached into her juju bag and took out a magic lotion and sprayed it over the monster river. In a twinkling the river dried up only inches away from the Niger, and the monster turned once again into a hippopotamus.

At this very moment Fara Maka appeared, worried about his dear daughter. Kara-Digi-Mao-Fosi-Fasi was by his side. And when the monster saw the two men, it forgot about the mere girl who was bothering it and charged at them, passing right by Nana Miriam.

Nana Miriam reached out, grabbed the hind leg of the hippopotamus, and picked the monster up. Twirling it three times around her head—remember, she was very strong!—she threw the monster across the Niger, which was, as luck would have it, not in flood at the time.

The monster smashed into a cliff of rocks on the other shore. Its skull cracked wide open. And so the rocks killed it; it was not killed by a human being.

Fara Maka held out his arms and Nana Miriam ran into them. "What a wonderful daughter I have," he said.

"What a wonderful papa I have," said Nana Miriam.

When they returned to the village, their story preceded them, for Kara-Digi-Mao-Fosi-Fasi had reported all that he had seen. There was singing and dancing, and feasting, as well.

And from that time to this, no Songhai have starved because of monster hippopotamuses. And from that day to this, the minstrels and storytellers have sung and told about Nana Miriam, who showed all the power of a mere girl!

GERMANY

Fitcher's Bird

*In the face of real evil, the hero must
use brains as well as brawn*

IN OLD COLOGNE, a city of stone houses and soft hearts, there lived
a widower with three handsome daughters: Gretchen, Gretel, and Erna.
What hard workers they were—up before the sun rose, and working from
dawn to dusk.

Near to Cologne, but not within its borders, there lived a wizard. Some
would say he was the devil himself. He often came into the city, dressed
like a beggar, going door to door and asking for bread. And each time—
though no one knew quite how—he managed to entice young maidens to
go with him. And not a one of them was ever seen again.

Now, one day this devilish beggar came calling at the widower's house.
He was dressed in a raggedy gray cloak. He had a raggedy gray cap. His
beard was silvery gray. And perhaps—yes, perhaps—he had cloven
hooves where his feet should have been, though one could not see them
for the rags.

Gretchen answered the door.

"Some bread for an old man?" the beggar asked in a quavering voice, holding up a leather bag. And when Gretchen gave bread to him, he touched her hand and—by magic—she was forced to jump into his sack.

Then away he went, away from the city, silently, mile after mile after mile—past villages and farms, up hills and down dales, across rivers and mountains. And if she spoke not a word, he was just as silent.

Finally they reached a great wooden house in the middle of a dark wood, where he let her out of the bag. The house was a mansion, with seven turrets but only one door.

"You shall be happy here in my house, where you shall be in charge of all my things," said the beggar, throwing off his raggedy cloak. And underneath he was clothed all in black, with silver buttons and golden toggles. But the splendor of his clothing did not disguise the fact that he was old, with wrinkles beneath his eyes and a snake's smile. And besides, he smelled of some awful wickedness.

Nevertheless, Gretchen was happy with her lot: a great man as her master and a great house to rule. It was much more than she could have even dreamed of in Cologne.

The wizard led Gretchen through the door and into the mansion, pointing to one room and then another. At the entrance to each room, he selected a different ornate key from a heavy ring of keys and handed it to her, saying, "Open the door, girl," which she did.

Each room was more beautiful than the last.

But when they came to the very last door, the wizard pointed to a small, unimportant-looking key that was tarnished and stained. "Do not ever use this key and do not ever open this door, my girl, on pain of death," the wizard said, then handed her the ring of keys.

"I will do as you say, master," Gretchen replied.

"That is good," said the wizard. "And one more thing." He reached into his pocket and produced an enormous pearly white egg. "Take this and keep it safe always. Otherwise misfortune will follow you."

It seemed an odd request, but no odder than her master, so Gretchen nodded.

"Good," the wizard said again. "Then I am off now to do my business." And he left her alone in the house.

Gretchen spun round and round, unable to believe her good fortune.

"Why, just this morning," she told herself, "I worked from dawn to dusk for very little recompense. But now I have all that I could ever want or need."

Quickly she found the dining room and sat down at the great banquet table, where she was served a fine supper by invisible hands. She drank red wine and had a lemon cake after. Then she went upstairs to sleep in a bed with a canopy of silk that shimmered like the night and stars.

IN THE MORNING, rising late, Gretchen once more ate alone, the great egg carefully set by the side of her plate. And as she ate she fingered the ring of keys. "I know what is in all the other rooms," she said to herself—speaking out loud because there was no one to hear her. "But I do not know what is in that last room." And soon her curiosity overcame her good sense, and she was convinced that if she was very careful, the wizard would never know she had peeked in.

Carrying the precious egg, she walked down the long hall to the last door and found the small stained key on the ring. Then she inserted the key into the lock and turned it. The door opened easily.

The room smelled like her master, of some awful wickedness. It was only half lit. But when, in that gray light, she saw a large tub in the center of the room, her curiosity impelled her to go over and peer in.

What a mistake! The tub was filled with the cut-up bodies of dead girls, who stared at her with sightless eyes.

Gretchen screamed and dropped the egg into the tub, and though she quickly drew it out again, it had become stained with blood.

She ran out of the room, slammed the door shut, and locked it again. Then she went directly to a great sink in the kitchen and rubbed and scrubbed at the egg. But hard as she tried to clean it, the blood would not come off.

WHEN THE WIZARD came home from his business, he asked to see the egg and knew at once what had happened.

"So, you have disobeyed me, Gretchen," he said. "You have entered the chamber against my wishes. Now you shall enter it against your own." He snatched her up by the hair and marched down the hall, swinging her back and forth, back and forth. When he got to the bloody chamber, he cut her up and flung her into the tub with the other girls.

The very next day the wizard went back to Cologne, in his beggar's disguise, and knocked on the widower's door.

This time it was Gretel who answered.

When she, too, gave him a piece of bread, he touched her hand, and into his leather bag she went.

And when they got to his house, what had happened to her poor sister happened to her, as well. Keys, egg, and the bloody chamber. Her curiosity overcame her prudence, and when the old wizard returned from his business, her life, too, was forfeit.

THE VERY NEXT DAY the old wizard appeared again as a beggar at the widower's house. This time it was Erna who answered the door.

Although she was more prudent than her sisters—and a bit sly, as well—she, too, gave the raggedy old beggar-man a bit of bread, and he popped her into his leather bag. And if anyone had watched how he walked, they might have noticed that he trod only on the tips of his toes, as if he had hooves and not human feet. Or they might have noticed how the back of his long beggar's cloak swished back and forth, as if there was a tail underneath. Or they might have seen how he kept his gray beggar's hat pulled down over his forehead, as if to hide a pair of horns. But no one was there to see.

When they got to his mansion, Erna, too, was shown around the place, room by room by room. She received the same warning as her sisters. She paid attention to the warning *and* to the way it was given. Thoughtfully she fingered the egg and the little key.

And when she woke in the morning, under the shimmering canopy, she said to herself, "Nothing the devil does is without meaning, though goodness only knows why he has given me this egg. Still, I had better keep it safe." She kneaded her pillow into a nest and placed the egg carefully in it. "Now I shall take a look at that mysterious door."

Quietly she went down the hall. Cautiously she unlocked the door. And when she opened the half-lit bloody chamber and saw her sisters lying in the tub in pieces, she knew what the devil was about.

But she collected herself and tenderly took out the pieces of her sisters' bodies and placed them in their proper positions on the floor. She was not entirely surprised when the pieces united together and the girls were once again whole and alive.

How they kissed and hugged and rejoiced then!

"But swiftly," Erna said, "you must hide, and I must find a way to fool that old devil." For remember—she was both prudent and sly.

WHEN THE WIZARD returned and asked to see the egg, he was delighted that it was smooth and unstained.

"And why not?" Erna asked. "Why would I not give you back the egg in the same condition you gave it to me?"

The devil had no answer for that, so he said only, "Because you have done what I asked, you shall be my bride. And as your husband, I must do anything you require."

"I wish it to be so with all my heart," said Erna. "And I have but one requirement."

"And what is that, my girl?" asked the wizard.

"You must carry a basket of gold to my poor father, who has had no word of me. And you must carry it yourself, not in your beggar's clothing but dressed as you are now, all handsome and rich."

The wizard preened with pride. If the girl said he was handsome, why, handsome he must be. There is no fool like an old devil. "If that is all, I shall be glad to visit him tomorrow."

"That is very kind of you," said Erna. "I only hope the basket will not be too heavy."

"Oh, do not worry about that," said the wizard, and he shifted a bit on his strange feet. "I can carry anything under the sun—and under the moon, as well—and not get tired."

Then Erna told him she had many preparations to make for the wedding and that a groom must not see the bride but once before the wedding.

Agreeing, the old wizard left her alone.

Erna waited until she heard the wizard's footsteps fade away down the hall. Then she signaled her two sisters to her.

"We are not out of the fire yet," Erna warned them. "You must do as I tell you."

She put them both in a large basket and covered them entirely with layers of gold coins. "You must keep very still," she said, "and that devil himself will carry you home. But this you must do: Any time he stops to put the basket down, you must cry out, 'I see you! I see you!'"

Gretchen and Gretel promised Erna they would do as she asked.

"Then, once you are safely home, pray send some help for me."

THE OLD WIZARD returned in the morning, resplendent in black, with silver buttons and golden toggles. He had a great black plumed hat on his head.

Erna greeted him at her bedroom door.

"Will you keep your word?" she asked.

"That I always do," he replied.

So she showed him the great basket with the gold coins winking and twinkling. "Remember your promise, and do not stop along the way."

"Do you not trust me?" asked the wizard, tilting his head to one side and trying to give her a trustworthy smile. It only made him look more like a snake.

"Of course," said Erna, returning him smile for smile. "For I have this one special ability: I can see from very very far away. If you dare stop and put that bag down, I will know!"

Off the old wizard went. Mile after mile after mile. It was sweaty work, even for such a devil. When he was only halfway there, he thought to rest a bit and so set the basket down.

But no sooner had he put the basket on the ground than one of the sisters in the basket cried out, "I am looking through my little window and I see you idling! I see you!"

"Ah, by the flames, it is true!" the wizard said. "She *can* see what I do!" So he hefted the basket at once and trotted quickly along the path to Cologne. But soon he tired again and set the basket down.

Then the other sister cried out, "I am looking through my little window and I see you idling! I see you!"

So he grabbed up the heavy basket again. And this time he did not stop till he got to Cologne and delivered the prize to the widower's door.

IN THE MEANTIME Erna had ordered the wedding feast and had invited friends of the wizard's, whose names were on a long list by the door.

Then taking the great egg, she covered it with a veil and ornaments and a crown of flowers. She carried it to the topmost window of the house, where she set it on a pillow on a chair and placed it as if it were looking out.

Everything being ready, she went downstairs again, this time to the kitchen, and dipped herself in a cask of honey. Then, after cutting open a featherbed, she rolled and rolled about in it till she was entirely covered with feathers and looked like some kind of marvelous bird.

Out of the house she went, and along the road she met some of the wedding guests—wizards and warlocks and witches all.

"Who are you?" asked the guests. "Are you Fitcher's bird?" Fitcher was one of the most important wizards.

"Yes," Erna cried, making her voice high and squawking. "I go to seek my lord."

"Is the bride ready?" asked the guests.

"Yes—" Erna said, "and she looks out the topmost window for the bridegroom."

The guests all waved at the window and went on into the house.

Now, some little ways down the road, Erna met the old wizard himself. He was walking slowly, glad to no longer be carrying his heavy burden. When he met Erna he did not recognize her at all but asked, "Are you Fitcher's bird?"

"Yes," squawked Erna. "I go to meet my lord."

"And is the bride ready?" asked the old wizard.

"From her head to her feet," Erna said. "She looks from the window abroad."

"Ah, well I know how she can see from that window," said the old wizard, rubbing his back. And he went on into the house.

But before he could see that the bride was no bride at all—but merely an egg dressed in a veil and crown—the men of Cologne who had been called out by the two sisters had arrived. They barred the one door, and then they set fire to the wizard's great house. So the wizard and all his wicked company were consumed in the flames.

As for Erna and her sisters and their father, they stayed on in Cologne, and the gold in the basket let them live together in comfort and happiness till the very end of their days.

ARGENTINA

The Girl and the Puma

There are many ways to be a hero—
muscle and magic are not the only roads

ONCE, LONG AGO—about four hundred years, to be exact—the great city of Buenos Aires was nothing more than a small Spanish settlement set in the heart of a wild and beautiful land.

But *los indios*, Indians who had lived there for more years than could be counted, had a great hatred for the Spaniards. The settlers had not only taken their land but had enslaved their people.

So, the battles raged on, up and down the green land, and the Indians at last laid siege to the little colony, encircling it with their warriors so that no one could get in with more supplies.

Inside the fort the settlers began to starve. They were reduced to eating rats, frogs, roots, even the leather from their boots. Some turned to cannibalism, devouring the flesh of those people who had died before them. Only a few soldiers tried to make it outside to hunt for food—and one by one they were captured and killed by the Indians.

So, the captain, Francisco Ruiz Galán, gave orders that no one else should try to leave—except by his permission. Anyone disobeying his orders would be hanged.

"Hanged or dead by starvation!" cried one young woman, who was called Señorita Maldonada, the "cursed señorita." "Is this a choice?" Even with the face of hunger stretched tight over her bones, she still had a formidable beauty. "I would rather hang with a full belly than die hungry."

So, in the afternoon, when everyone in the fort dozed in the heat, she slipped out of the fort and crawled through the high grasses. The Indians must have been dozing, too, for no one stopped her. She made it all the way to Punta Gorda and the margin of the river, where she found old fruit beneath the trees. She devoured it all and looked around for more.

By the time she had eaten her fill, it was twilight. She knew then a sudden great fear: fear of being caught by the Indians, or of being eaten by wild animals, or of being hung by her own people.

Perhaps, she thought, *if I can bring back some kind of food to the fort I will be forgiven.* But what kind of food? She had eaten everything she had found so far. And as night came on, she began to cry.

But then she pulled herself upright. "Crying will not feed any bellies." She determined to be brave. "I must shelter for the night and search for more food in the early morn."

So, she found a cave not far from the river and crept in.

GRRRRRRRRR. A DEEP, rumbling growl greeted her. She saw two green eyes, like gems, glaring at her.

When her eyes grew used to the dark, she realized what it was.

"Holy Mother, a puma!" she whispered, and felt faint. Could she possibly outrun the beast?

But then she saw that the puma had just given birth to a cub and seemed in great pain. There was another cub to be born, but it was stuck in the birth canal. The puma whimpered and lay back down, exhausted.

What makes a hero? Is it being brave, or is it acting while being greatly afraid? Señorita Maldonada did something incredibly courageous. She tore a strip from her skirt and cleaned off the newborn cub of its birth matter. Then she helped the puma with the last cub, just as she had helped women giving birth in the fort.

FOR DAYS AFTER, Señorita Maldonada stayed in the cave with the puma and her cubs, sharing the food the mother puma brought back. Sometimes Señorita Maldonada herself went out and found fruits and berries for them all.

Did she remember the fort? Of course.

But her concern was for her animal family now.

AND THEN ONE DAY, when she was out by the river drinking water, a band of Querandi Indians saw her and captured her and marched her back to their village.

They fed her and, recognizing her gentle beauty, kept her as a member of the tribe. She learned their language, worked alongside their women on the small farm plots, married one of the men, and was content.

Did she remember the fort? Of course.

Did she remember the pumas? Of course.

But her concern was for her Indian family now.

AND THEN ONE DAY, when the men were out hunting and the women were left to do the chores, a band of Spaniards from the fort suddenly appeared, for they had broken through the siege.

The Querandi women and children fled, but Señorita Maldonada did

not. She greeted them in Spanish, and they recognized her, though she was dressed as an Indian.

They brought her back to the fort and she was immediately surrounded by the people, who were amazed that she was still alive.

Captain Ruiz Galán looked at her in her Indian dress, her face no longer a mask of hunger. "You knew my orders," the captain said. "You disobeyed them. You will hang."

"I was dying of hunger," she answered.

"We were all dying of hunger," the captain said. "Orders are orders."

Señorita Maldonada looked right at him. "You are crueler than the puma," she said. "Crueler than *los indios*. We take from them and kill them without thinking, yet they took me in and made me their own."

"Nevertheless you must hang," said the captain.

An angry buzz ran around the crowd, and the captain, sensing a mutiny, quickly gave in. "I will show you that I, too, can be kind. I will not hang her. Let her be tied to a tree outside. Then we will see how kindly the wild beasts and Indians treat her."

Señorita Maldonada made no word of protest. She understood kindness now. And courage. She would trust to her God and her friends.

SO, IT WAS DONE. They took her to a tree some five kilometers from the town. No one was allowed to go and help her for three days. But then, knowing that she was surely dead, the people begged to bring back her body for burial, and a detail of soldiers went out to fetch back her remains.

But when they got to the tree, there was a great puma and two cubs guarding the girl, who was alive and unharmed.

"Is it a ghost?" cried one soldier.

Another fell to his knees.

Señorita Maldonada raised her eyes to them. "My puma let no other beast near me. She brought me fruits and berries to eat. She cleansed me with her great tongue. But she is an animal and could not free me."

The soldiers untied her and brought her back to the colony. There they renamed her Señorita Biendonada, the "blessed señorita," and begged Captain Ruiz Galán to be as kind to her as the beasts had been.

What else could he do?

He let her stay. And she outlived him by many years, helping in the founding of the city of Asunción and giving her name to the city Maldonado in Uruguay, across the Río de la Plata.

Do you believe this story?

Only if you believe in kindness and in courage.

CHINA

Li Chi Slays the Serpent

Here is a maiden who will not be sacrificed!

ONCE, LONG AGO, in a cleft in the northwest portion of the great Yung Mountains, there lived a giant serpent. He was many *lis* long, and to span his body would have taken ten hands.

If the serpent had remained only in the cleft, eating rabbits and mice and an occasional deer, no one would have thought anything of it. Serpents often dwelled in the mountains in those days.

But this serpent had crept down into the valley on moonless nights and taken off first sheep, then oxen, and finally it almost swallowed a magistrate's daughter who was visiting the home of an elderly aunt, though she managed to escape and run home.

The local people became terrified. Wouldn't you be, if a gigantic serpent, larger than a tree, was devouring your livestock and threatening a child?

So, the villagers sent word to the military commander of the nearby capital city. And, as is often the case, he was a friend of the magistrate whose daughter had been nearly devoured.

The commander sent out soldiers to slay the dragon. Ten men marched out—and only one marched back. The rest had been eaten by the monster, who now had a taste for human flesh.

The serpent made its desires known through the dreams of mediums and charlatans and seers.

"Bring me a sweet and succulent young maiden," the serpent told them. "No more soldiers, if you please. They are too tough and not particularly pleasant. Once a year, on the eighth day of the eighth month, deliver the girl to my cave. If you do so, I will leave your flocks and soldiers alone."

Helpless, the commander and the magistrate consulted with the most important men of the city and the villages nearby. At last, reluctantly, they decided they had no choice. So they began selecting the daughters of criminals and servants, one a year, for nine years. With bound hands and feet, the girls were delivered to the cleft in the rock that was the serpent's cave.

Nine years.

Nine girls.

IN THE TENTH YEAR the men began once again their search for the perfect sweet and succulent maiden, to have her bound and ready for the eight month.

Now, there was a man in the countryside below the Yung Mountains named Li Tan. He had six daughters and no sons. His youngest daughter—Li Chi—came to him as the search went on.

"Father," she said, "let me be the girl sent to the serpent."

Li Tan refused.

His wife refused.

"We will not let you die in the mouth of this monster," they said.

Li Chi bowed to them. "Dear parents," she said, "since you have brought forth six daughters and no sons, it is as if you were childless. I am nothing. I am the sixth nothing in this family." (For in those days girls were considered of no value in a Chinese family.)

"You are not 'nothing' to us," said her parents.

"Nevertheless, I cannot take care of you when you are old," Li Chi continued. "I only waste your food and clothing. What would be wrong in selling me to the serpent seekers and getting a bit of money for yourselves?"

But her parents would not let her go. So Li Chi sneaked out of the house that very night and, in secret, presented herself to the authorities.

"But do not bind my hands and feet," she said. "Give me, rather, a sharp sword and a snake-hunting dog."

"What can you, a mere girl, do that ten men could not?" they asked.

"What does it matter if I go armed or unarmed?" asked Li Chi.

"You are right," said the authorities. "The serpent will have you in the end." And they gave her a sharp sword and the best serpent-hunting dog that could be found, for they were relieved not to have to search further.

WHEN THE EIGHTH DAY of the eighth month arrived, Li Chi readied herself. She took several pecks of rice balls moistened with malt sugar and put them in a sack. Then, with the sack over her left shoulder and the sword over her right, she whistled up the dog and started up the steep Yung Mountains. Soldiers trailed behind her to make certain that she did not turn back.

All day she climbed without stopping, and never a word she spoke to the men.

At last she came to the serpent's cave and only then turned to the captain of the troop. "Take your men back," she said. "It would not do to have them be eaten."

The men were grateful to leave.

As soon as they were out of sight, Li Chi got out the rice balls and put them at the mouth of the cave, lined up one on top of the other.

"Oh serpent!" she called. "Eat these sweet rice balls and not poor pitiful me." And she wept loudly, as if she were afraid.

The serpent, smelling both the rice balls and the succulent girl, slithered out of the cave, headfirst. And that head was as large as a barrel.

"I shall eat the rice balls, and then I shall eat you, as well," it hissed.

Opening its mouth wide to bite down on the sticky balls, the serpent momentarily obscured its own eyesight. That was the very moment Li Chi unleashed the snake-hunting dog.

The dog made no distinction between a small adder and a great serpent, and it bit hard on the back of the serpent's neck.

The serpent tried to shake off the dog but could not.

Then Li Chi came up from behind with the sword and scored deep gashes into the serpent's neck.

At this the serpent tried to back up and could not, so deep and awful were its wounds. So it tried instead to slide out farther to give itself more room to fight. But at each new length of its body, Li Chi struck with the sword and the snake-hunting dog bit with its sharp teeth.

And very soon the serpent was bloodied all over. And very soon after that, it shook all over. And then it died.

Li Chi waited until she was certain the serpent was dead, and then she went into the cave, where she found the skulls of the nine girls. She sighed, brought them out one by one by one, and put them into the sack, saying, "For your timidity you were devoured. How pitiful that is."

Then she went back down the mountain path, with the snake-hunting dog trotting behind.

It is said that the king of Yueh learned of these events from a ballad singer and made Li Chi his queen. It is further said that he appointed Li Tan as his chief magistrate of the district around the Yung Mountains. Li Chi's mother was given many honors, and her sisters were married off to noblemen. In this way, the girls brought honor and riches to the family.

And from that day to this—owing to the power and determination of one girl—the Yung Mountains have been free of monster serpents.

UNITED STATES/WHITE RIVER SIOUX

Brave Woman Counts Coup

The Sioux believe this to be a true story,
but it has many elements of a folktale

NOW, NOT ALL STORIES take place in the once-upon-a-time. This one happened less than two hundred years ago, when the Sioux lived in what is now Minnesota. The chief of this particular people was called Tawa Makoce, which means "his country."

In his youth Tawa Makoce was a good leader and a great warrior. As a man he married and had three sons and a daughter. When he no longer went out fighting with the young men, he proved a wise voice in the council.

To have such a strong man for a father can be hard on the sons. And so it was with the sons of Tawa Makoce. They wanted to prove themselves worthy of him, and this made them reckless in battle. One by one by one they died fighting their enemies, the Crow.

Soon only the daughter, Makhta, was left.

Makhta was beautiful and proud. Not proud as some beautiful women are, strutting and preening and showing themselves off. And not so proud that she did not do the work that was expected of her. But proud within.

38

She carried herself bravely in spite of losing her brothers, and she swore that she would never marry until she herself counted coup on the murderous Crow.

Now, a woman of the Sioux does not ordinarily count coup, does not ride into the enemy camp and touch them with a coup stick, showing contempt for their ability to fight. But this is what Makhta said: "I will ride with the warriors of our people to the very cook fires of the Kangi Oyate, the Crow nation."

The men did not believe her, of course. They knew what a woman should do and what she should not. A woman cooked the food. A woman made the moccasins. A woman skinned the buffalo and stretched the hides. A woman did not count coup.

Makhta was a beautiful woman, so, many of the young men had sent their fathers to her father with gifts of horses to show that they wished to make Makhta their wife. Red Horn, son of a chief, made his father go not once and not twice but three time to ask for Makhta in marriage.

But each time Makhta said no.

Now, there was one young man who desired her, as well, but he was too shy to say it, and too poor to make an offer for her. His name was Little Eagle and he only loved Makhta from afar.

But even had she known of his love, Makhta would still have said no. Until her brothers were given their honor, until she could count coup for them, she would not marry.

IT HAPPENED THAT the Crow, the Kangi Oyate, had moved onto lands that the White River Sioux believed were their own. So the young Sioux men decided to ride out in a war party and chase the Crows away.

Makhta put on her best dress of white buckskin, with moccasins to match. She put on a necklace of shells. And thus dressed, she went to speak to her father.

"My father," she said, "now is the time I can do what I have promised. I will go with these warriors to the place where our enemy lives, and there I will count coup for my brothers' honor. Give me permission to go."

Did he want to let her go? Of course not. Would he let her go? He saw her pride. Then he wept and said, "You are my last child. I see that I must go into my old age without children and without grandchildren around me. But you must ride. You have said it. Take my warbonnet and wear it, remembering your brothers."

SO, MAKHTA TOOK the warbonnet and gathered her brothers' weapons— the bows and arrows they had made with such loving care, the lance, the shield, the war club. She took her father's best war pony. Then, renamed Brave Woman by her father, she mounted and rode with the young men toward the river, the Big Muddy, the Missouri.

Did the young men want her to go? Of course not. Red Horn was furious. Little Eagle was afraid. But she had gotten her father's permission; she wore his warbonnet. They could not send her away.

So, they rode and rode for many days, gathering Sioux warriors from other villages as they went.

When they came at last to a hill overlooking the Crow village, it seemed as if the entire Crow nation—hundreds of men, thousands of horses—were waiting for them.

"Should we go back?" one young man asked.

"I have come to count coup to honor my brothers," said Makhta. "I will not leave without doing so. Who will ride on with me?"

Red Horn nodded. "I will."

She handed him her oldest brother's lance and shield.

"I will," said Little Eagle.

Makhta gave him her second brother's bow and arrows.

"I will," said another young man, and to him Makhta gave her youngest brother's war club.

"We all will!" shouted the rest.

"But what will *you* use?" asked Little Eagle.

Makhta smiled and took her father's curved coup stick wrapped in otter skin from her belt. "I will count coup with this. I am my father's strong right arm."

And then she began a war chant, high and trembling. It put heart into the young warriors, and they turned with their horses and charged down into the midst of the boil of Crow.

But the Sioux were so few and the Crow were so many, soon the young Sioux warriors were being beaten back.

That was when Makhta kicked her father's old war pony in the flanks with her heels and headed him right into the thick of the fight. All the while she kept singing that high, shrill war chant.

One, two—she reached out with the otter-fur coup stick, so close that she could easily count the four eagle feathers in one warrior's hair, could see the bunches of crow feathers on another's black-handled spear. When they saw her in the very midst of the battle, new heart was put into the Sioux warriors and they turned back again and renewed the fight.

But once more the Sioux were beaten, overwhelmed by the number of enemies. This time a musket ball hit the old war pony in the chest. It fell to its knees and Makhta was tumbled onto the ground. Still, standing, she reached up to count coup, on a foot here, a leg there, as the Crow warriors battled around her.

Red Horn rode by her, but he did not stop to help, for he was busy in the fight.

Then Little Eagle rode over to her and got off his pony. He helped her mount up. He slapped the horse with her brother's bow, and the pony—

wounded and weary—bolted, taking Makhta out of the center of the battle and to a place of safety.

From that position, Makhta rallied the rest of the Sioux for one last charge. And this time such was their fury—and such was their pride—that they drove the Crow away: away from the camp and away from the Missouri forever.

But Little Eagle, on foot in the very red center of the fight, had taken a killing blow to the face. Makhta found him there, her brother's bow still in his hand.

"Let us build a scaffold for him here—here where he died a true warrior," said Makhta. "He honored my brothers and he honored the Sioux. He helped save our nation forever." She drew her knife across her arms and legs till the blood ran, and cut slashes in her buckskin dress as a sign of deep mourning.

The other warriors slew Little Eagle's poor wounded pony to serve him in the Land of Many Lodges.

When they all returned home, Red Horn was in disgrace for his part in the battle, for many of his companions had seen his refusal to help Makhta. He could not even look at her after that.

But Makhta did not notice. As she told her father, "You are to call me Little Eagle's widow, for in the heat of battle, we were wed in blood. I will mourn him as long as I mourn my brothers."

So, Makhta won the honor and respect of her people, and she held to her promise, mourning Little Eagle till the day she died.

UNITED STATES/OZARKS

Pretty Penny

*Sometimes a quick wit is faster
than a pointed gun*

WELL, THERE WAS ONCE a man named Old Jake who had a daughter named Penny—about sixteen years old, she was, and round and shiny as her name, with long dark plaits and a button nose.

Old Jake wasn't a man to work hard. He just loaned out money at a high interest. And he didn't trust anybody but his own daughter to bring that money home.

"Take care of the Penny," he would say, "and the dollars take care of themselves."

One day some folks over the east of town were ready to pay off their mortgage, and Old Jake sent Penny down the road to collect it. They gave her the hundred dollars they owed—which was a lot of money in those days—all in silver coins. She packed it up in a little paper sack, flung her plaits across her back, then headed for home.

Huppity-one, huppity-two, she walked on down the road, minding her manners and tending to her own business, when behind her she heard the *cloppity-clop* of a great big horse.

44

She moved to the roadside to let the horse and rider pass, but when they came by her and she looked up, she saw the rider was a road agent, a highway thief, with a red bandanna over his nose and mouth, and a pistol in his hand.

"Howdy, Miz Penny!" he called. He sure knew her, though she didn't know him.

He jumped off that horse and grabbed her round the waist. Near tore her dress off reaching for her tote sack.

"Give me that, girl!" he cried.

She kicked and hollered and punched him; she slapped him with those thick dark plaits, but it was no good. She was a big girl, but he was a bigger man.

When she saw he was getting the better of her, she tore open that sack and scattered the silver dollars all over the road.

That road agent dropped her like she was a hot pan just off the fire, and began to scrabble around picking up the coins. Which was just what Penny was hoping.

Without a moment's hesitation, she jumped onto his big horse, kicking it hard with her heels. Then off she rode to her pappy's house.

Well, the road agent got up off his knees and fired off one shot from his pistol. But he was too late. Penny was like the wind in a holler: hot and fast and gone.

When she got home, Old Jake looked at her on that high horse. "What do you mean, riding around like a hoyden, your dress half tore off and the hair coming out of your plaits? And where is the tote sack full of my mortgage money?"

Penny climbed off the horse, settled her dress to be more ladylike, bound up her plaits once more, and told him what had happened. Then she said, "Look in the saddlebags, Pappy."

And what do you think he found?

Gold and silver, silver and gold. All that the road agent had stolen in a year.

"Daughter," Old Jake admitted, "you have worked harder this day than I have ever seen. There's a hundred times more money in these saddlebags than was ever in that tote sack. You kept your honor, and your pappy's as well."

"And I got us a good horse, and a saddle, too," Penny pointed out.

Did they keep what they got?

Well, who was to tell on them? Not that road agent. He couldn't say where he had happened on all that money. And there was a price on his head besides.

Some say it shows that honesty pays off in the long run. Not me. I'd rather say a Penny goes a long way on the road to riches. And a quick-thinking Penny can be the start of a vast fortune.

SCOTLAND

Burd Janet

Sometimes to be a hero means holding on;
sometimes it means letting go

ONCE, ON A WEEDY PIECE of land called Carterhaugh, there was a strange, forbidding castle. It had been many years since anyone had lived in the place. Only the rats and mice and owls claimed it for a home.

"Do not go down to Carterhaugh," warned the mothers and fathers of the lands around. "It is a place of evil. Do not go there. The Fair Folk"—and by this they meant the trooping fairies—"own it now."

Most of the children heeded the warnings, but for a few of the more adventurous boys—and they went down to Carterhaugh only on dares. They would go and leave a token, then hurry home again. But not a one of them ever went a second time.

Now, there was one girl, the clan chief's lass—called Janet by her mother but affectionately called Burd Janet by her nanny—who laughed at the warnings when they came to her in turn. "I am not afraid," she said. "My father's father's father owned Carterhaugh. It is mine by right, though I am not allowed to claim it. When I am old enough, I shall go there and take it for my own."

Her mother and father wept to hear her talk that way, for she was their only child and they loved her dearly. "Do not go," they begged.

But Janet had always had a mind of her own, even as a wee girl. The villagers all said she would never be wed, not with that temperament, even though her father was the chief of the clan. When Burd Janet said, "I will go to Carterhaugh," no one doubted it was all but done.

THE YEARS PASSED and Burd Janet turned sixteen, coming into her inheritance. Downstairs her family and friends had gathered to wish her well. A fiddle was scratching away, and a piper played the old tunes of glory. Burd Janet twisted her red-gold hair into a braid and fastened it atop her head. She put on her birthday gown, green as young willow. She pinned on a great length of her clan's tartan. Then off she went down the backstairs, without being seen, and headed to Carterhaugh, leaving the singing, dancing guests behind.

The night drew in soft around her, but the road grew rocky the closer she came to the river Yarrow. At the last she left the road, kirtled her long skirts above her knees, and bounded over the heathery hills toward the tumbledown towers of Carterhaugh. She had only the moon to light her way.

When she got to the old castle, it was fully dark. Night birds called from the trees. The shadows of briars seemed sharper than the briars themselves. And the only spot of color there, besides Burd Janet herself, was a single red rose blooming from a thorny bush by the door.

Burd Janet was afraid, but she would not show it. "Hullo, the house!" she called out in greeting. "Tonight I have come into my inheritance. By law I claim what is mine. This house and land belonged to my father's father's father, though it was stolen from him by the wickedness of the Fair Folk."

There was a sudden rush of wind as if in answer, but nothing more.

Burd Janet smiled. "I shall take this single rose, the only thing left of beauty here at the hall. And I leave instead my pledge. I shall take back Carterhaugh from the fairies and restore it to humankind."

Then she plucked the rose, though the thorns pierced her fingers and made them bleed.

No sooner had the stalk been broken than the wind blew up again, now wild and angry. The moon was suddenly hidden by a shred of cloud. And when the cloud was past, standing in front of her, where no one had been a moment before, was the handsomest young man Burd Janet had ever seen. He was dressed as if for a wedding, with a fine kilt, a silken shirt, a velvet jacket, a silver-handled *skean dhu* tucked into his sock, and a silver *sporran* hanging from his waist.

"Who pulls the rose?" he said in a voice that was both soft and strong. "Who calls me back from the world of the Ever Fair?"

Janet laughed. "I pulled the rose," she said. "And the world of the Ever Fair is but a dream. No one lives forever. We all grow old in time."

The young man put his head to one side and looked at her. "So I once believed, too. But as I rode out on a summer's eve, my horse shied and I fell off. As I lay in a faint on the hillside, the queen of the Fair Folk found me and took me inside the green hill. And I have lived there ever since. Never growing older. Never dying."

"How long is 'ever since'?" asked Burd Janet. "You do not look older than I am, and today is my sixteenth birthday."

"I am ten times sixteen, older than the oldest man left outside the hill," the young man replied.

Janet laughed again. "I cannot believe that. What is your name, sir?"

"My name is Tam Lin."

And then Burd Janet shivered for the first time, for Tam Lin was the name of a boy who had disappeared when her father's father's father was a boy.

"When I rode off, this house stood upright and unbroken," said Tam Lin. "The flowers bloomed all across the hill."

"They shall bloom here again," said Burd Janet. "And the towers shall once again stand tall. For I am Burd Janet and this is my house and land."

"That I should like to see," said Tam Lin, and he took Burd Janet's hand and kissed it.

"I promise you shall," she said.

But at her words Tam Lin shivered, as if a cold wind had touched the back of his neck, though there was no wind at all. "After tomorrow—All Hallow's Eve—I shall see nothing ever again," he said. "For on that night, when the human and fairy worlds sit side by side, with only the moonlight road between, the queen of the Fair Folk plans to sacrifice me as a *teind* to Hell."

"Never!" said Burd Janet.

"There is naught anyone can do," said Tam Lin.

"There is always something..." she replied.

He shook his head. "We ride over the moors, past Selkirk town, down to Miles Cross, where the holy well stands, as the *unseelie* court does every seven years. And every seven years the queen sacrifices one of her human captives. For long she has loved me and kept me by her side. But now she loves another and I have been chosen to die."

"Can you refuse to ride, Tam Lin?"

"That I cannot."

"Can you run?"

"That I cannot."

"Is there no one to stand between?"

"Only my own true love," said Tam Lin. "But all who loved me are long dead, and the grass growing green over their graves."

"Then *I* shall save you!" cried Burd Janet. "For if no one else in this human world loves you, then I must."

He grabbed her up in his arms and told her what she must do. Then he kissed her twice, once on the lips and once on the forehead, before he let her go.

BURD JANET WENT BACK to her house. The party for her majority was still going on. If anyone had missed her, no one said a word. Her mother saw the scratches on her fingers. Her father saw the rose in her hand. But neither saw the mark of Tam Lin's kisses on her lips and forehead, though she felt them burning like brands.

She danced with young men who had fair faces and soft hands. She danced with young men who had dark faces and rough hands. But she danced with none who took her breath as did Tam Lin.

And so she bid them all good night.

In the morning she slept late, and her nanny wondered at the burrs in her skirts. The rose, which she had set in a vase, had wilted. But when Burd Janet arose, there was a blush on her cheek.

When evening came at last, she wrapped a green mantle over her head. In her leather pocket she carried earth from the garden, and a bottle of holy water begged from the priest. In her head were the instructions from Tam Lin.

She crept out of the house and ran down the road to Miles Cross, where she hid herself in back of the well. She knew she had a long while to wait.

Then, when the bell in the steeple of Selkirk town tolled twelve, she heard the jangling of many smaller bells, and so she made herself smaller still and watched the road without moving.

There, where the mist parted like a great gate opening, came the fairy troop. The sound Burd Janet had heard before was the horses' harnesses, for they were bridled in gold and silver, and hung all over with bells. On each horse's head shone a great jewel.

Burd Janet remembered all that Tam Lin had told her, and she let the first horse—the pitch black horse—pass her by. On its back was a man as fair as a prince.

And then she let the second horse—an oak brown horse—pass by as well. The man on its back was as fair as a king.

Then the third horse came by—white as milk, white as snow, white as the froth on the top of a wave. On its back rode Tam Lin.

Burd Janet leaped to her feet and ran over to the white horse, and with one swift movement, she pulled the rider down, holding him fast in her arms.

Even swifter was the fairy troop, for in an instant she and Tam Lin were surrounded.

Burd Janet looked up at the riders and saw that their faces were all beautiful but cold, and the coldest and most beautiful was the face of the Fairy Queen herself. Her dress was all the greens of the forest, and her white hair hung in a hundred braids down her back.

"Give me Tam Lin," said the Fairy Queen, "and I shall give you all the gold and silver you see here."

Tam Lin had not told Burd Janet what to say, for he had not known the queen would bargain for him. But Burd Janet never hesitated. "I have enough gold in my mother's hair and silver in my father's," she said.

"Give me Tam Lin," the Fairy Queen said again, "and I shall give you all the jewels on my horses' heads."

Burd Janet smiled. "I need only the jewels shining in my true love's eyes."

The Fairy Queen stared straight into Burd Janet's eyes as if reading what was written in her soul. "Give me Tam Lin," she said carefully, "and I shall give you back Carterhaugh."

For a moment—only a moment—Burd Janet hesitated. In her mind came images of the beauty of the house, not as it could be but as it had once been. Then she knew that the queen was trying to throw a glamour over her and she laughed.

"I shall have Carterhaugh whether you will it or no," Burd Janet told the queen. "And Tam Lin, as well."

The queen stood up in her silver stirrups and pointed a long finger at Burd Janet. "You do not hold him even now!" she cried. A great white light poured from her fingertips.

In Burd Janet's arms Tam Lin began to twist and shiver and groan. His flesh seemed to melt and then reshape itself into that of a green, sinuous, scaly serpent, with lidless eyes and a lipless smile.

But Burd Janet held on.

The Fairy Queen laughed without mirth. "What do you hold now, Burd Janet?"

The serpent shape melted in her hands and reshaped again, and now Burd Janet held a lion, whose great mouth was open and whose teeth were bared and whose breath smelled of dead meat.

But still Burd Janet held on.

"What do you hold now, human girl?" cried the queen.

The lion's body ran like molten gold through her hands and reshaped into a burning brand.

But heedless of the fire that seared her, Burd Janet held on, running to the well, where, at the very last moment, she threw the brand in. Then she took the bottle of holy water from her pocket and sprinkled it into the well and over her own head.

The brand went out at once, and Tam Lin climbed out. His fairy clothing had been burned away and he stood in nothing but his human skin.

Burd Janet threw the green mantle around him to shade him from fairy sight. Then she reached back into the leather pocket and took out the earth from her garden. She spread it around the two of them in a great circle of protection against the Fair Folk.

Tam Lin took her hand in his, and they turned to face the queen.

"If I had known what I know now, Tam Lin, I would have plucked out your human eyes and given you eyes of wood!" cried the Fairy Queen. But as she spoke, the sun was just rising above the rim of the world.

"Your power is over," Burd Janet cried out. "For here is the daylight and Tam Lin is mine!"

The queen turned to look at the sun creeping down the road like some unearthly beast on the prowl. "We must be gone!" she cried in a voice that trilled with terror.

"Be gone!" the *unseelie* court answered her.

Then the queen and court rode silently away through the gates of mist, leaving Tam Lin and Burd Janet behind.

BURD JANET AND TAM LIN were married. They took back the great castle of Carterhaugh and lived there with their children, and their children's children, for many long and happy years. As happy and as even, it is said, as the bones of the herring on either side of the spine.

ROMANIA

Mizilca

*Young women disguising themselves as men to go off
to battle are popular in folk stories as well as in history*

THERE WAS ONCE in far-off Romania a good old knight who was skilled at sorcery, but alas, he was failing in health. He had three beautiful daughters and no sons.

Now, the old knight loved his daughters mightily, but the youngest daughter, Mizilca, he loved the best.

One day the far-off sultan sent word to all the knights in his kingdom that they must, on pain of death and dishonor, come with horse and arms and serve him for a year and a day. Or failing that, they must send one of their sons to do the sultan's duty.

The old knight himself was too sick to travel. And, as has been said, he had no sons, so he did not know what to do. Day and night he worried about it, sighing deeply and refusing to eat. Soon his ill health became no health at all, and there came a day when he was all but on his deathbed.

His eldest daughter, Stanuta, came to him. She put a hand to his head, and the skin there felt hot and dry. "Dear father," she said, "what is wrong? Why do you sigh and fail to thrive?"

The knight sighed deeply, and the sides of his great mustache fluttered like wings. "The sultan has commanded me to come myself or send my son to serve at his court for a year and a day. If I cannot do so, I shall be dishonored, executed, and all my lands confiscated. Then what will happen to my dear daughters?"

Stanuta rose from his bedside and stood up tall. "I will be your son and go. Let my hair be cut off like a man's, give me a man's shirt and pants. Then I will ride astride a horse like a man and serve the sultan well."

The old man was horrified at the thought. He forbade his daughter to go to the sultan's court alone. The sultan's reputation with women was known throughout the land. But there was no dissuading Stanuta. So at last the old man had to agree.

Stanuta's maids cut off her long dark hair and dressed her like a boy. Her father gave her a suit of the finest armor and his sharpest sword, and had her mounted on his finest warhorse.

"Fair weather and fine roads, my son," the old knight said as she rode away.

But then the old knight did a very strange thing. He cut across the fields, though he was still very weak from his illness, and went as fast as ever he could until he came to a bridge at the very boundary of his lands. There, using a secret signal with his hands and a few magic words, he changed himself into a blue boar and hid in the woods by the river.

Stanuta came riding along on the warhorse and the blue boar charged out at her. He blew blue smoke through his nostrils and grunted a warning.

Stanuta's horse would have stood its ground, but Stanuta screamed in terror and pulled on the reins till it turned around. She galloped back to the castle so quickly, the old knight had barely time to transform himself and make it back ahead of her. The trip nearly finished him, and he lay down on his bed and barely moved for a week.

NOW, THE OLD KNIGHT'S second daughter, Roxanda, saw him lying and sighing in his bed, and she put her hand to his cheek. It was hot and dry. She asked, as had her sister before her, what was the matter. And, as her sister before her, she begged to go to the sultan's palace as the knight's own son.

"No blue boar shall turn me from my path," she swore.

So, her maids, too, cut her hair and dressed her as a man. She put on the suit of armor and mounted her father's good warhorse. Then off she went down the road.

But her old father arose from his bed of pain and was there ahead of her at the bridge, changed into the shape of a red lion.

When Roxanda reached the bridge, the red lion leaped forward and roared, its great teeth gnashing.

Roxanda, too, screamed in terror, pulled on the reins, and galloped home. Her old father had barely time to change back and make it home ahead of her.

NOW, OF COURSE, it was Mizilca's turn. She asked, as had her sisters before her, for her father's blessing to go to the sultan's palace as the knight's son.

"Dear Mizilca," her father said. "Your sisters, who are older and stronger than you, have failed. Stay home. Keep your long, lovely hair, which is truly your crowning glory."

"Father, I will not fail. Neither lion nor boar shall frighten me."

"No. Absolutely not," the old knight said. He worried less about the lion and boar, and more about the sultan. But if he thought that would be the end of it, he was wrong. Mizilca kept begging and begging until at last—to have a little peace—he let her go. But all he gave her was a rusty old sword, a broken old lance, and an old swaybacked horse that had done nothing but pull the farm cart for years.

As soon as Mizilca had cut her hair, put on armor, taken up the sword and lance, and started off, her father was across the fields and by the bridge in the magical likeness of a green dragon, waiting for her.

The minute Mizilca got to the bridge, out charged the dragon, snorting and roaring and blowing flames.

But Mizilca was not like her sisters. She put her spurs to the old sway-back's flanks and galloped forward. She lowered her lance to pierce the dragon's breast.

At that the dragon turned and ran off, back across the fields and out of sight. The poor old knight barely made it to his bed that day.

MIZILCA RODE STRAIGHT on to the sultan's palace, which was three days and three nights away.

When she arrived she bowed low before the sultan and said, "I am my father's son, and I have come to serve you for a year and a day, and thus discharge his debt to you."

The sultan checked her off in his great book of names, but then he looked her up and down, and thought to himself, *I know men and I know maidens. This is no youth, but a maiden disguised.* Yet, he was not entirely sure. And he did not dare say anything in case he was wrong. So he welcomed her to the company of his knights with open arms.

DAYS PASSED. WEEKS. And the sultan watched Mizilca closely. But she rode as well as any man. And she shot the bow as well as any man. She handled sword and lance as well as any man.

Yet still, he was not certain. He fretted about this, day and night, night and day, till his old mother asked him what was wrong.

"There is a knight among my knights whom I suspect is no man," he said. "How can I discover the truth without dishonor?"

His old mother smiled. "Ask me a harder question, my son. This one is too easy. Have merchants come to the palace and let them place rich cloths on one side of the great hall: embroidered silken shifts, intricate laces, long flowing veils, and velvet robes. On the other side of the great hall, have the merchants spread out armaments: fine two-sided swords, ivory-handled knives, carved lances, ebony spears."

The sultan nodded.

"Then," his mother continued, "if the knight is a maiden, she will be drawn to the cloth and pay no attention at all to the weapons."

The sultan did as his mother said, and all the knights were called into the great hall. But when Mizilca entered and saw what goods were laid out, she suspected at once what the sultan was about. So she ignored the embroideries, the silks, the laces, the veils. Instead she went straight to the weapons and hefted the swords.

But the sultan was still not convinced. Once again he asked his mother. "How can I discover whether Mizilca is a man or a maid without dishonor?"

His old mother smiled again. "Ask me a harder question, my son. This one is too easy. Have cook prepare kasha for dinner and mix in it a spoonful of pearls. If the knight is a maiden, she will pick out the pearls one by one and save them. If he is a man, he will throw the pearls away."

So, the knights were all invited to a grand feast, and the first course was kasha, and in each bowl were pearls mixed with the buckwheat grains.

Mizilca again suspected the sultan was testing her. And she picked out the pearls and flung them under the table as if they were nothing more than stones.

The sultan gnashed his teeth and shook his head but could prove nothing. So once again he asked his old mother's advice.

His old mother smiled. "Ask me a harder question, my son. This one is too easy. Spread peas on the floor of the great hall, and bring the knights

in. Women walk lightly and will scatter the peas. Men trod firmly and will crush them."

So, the sultan did as she advised, and peas were spread on the polished floor. But when the knights were called in, Mizilca once more saw what the sultan was up to and she trod firmly on the peas, making sure to crush them beneath her boots.

The sultan was enraged and banished his old mother to her rooms for a month, but he also gave up trying to discover Mizilca's secret. And so the year of service sped by.

AT LAST THE TIME came for Mizilca to go home. She said farewell to the men with whom she had served, and had just mounted her old sway-backed horse when the sultan himself came out to say good-bye.

He stood by the horse's side and looked at Mizilca for a long moment without a word. Then at last he said, "You have served me well, Mizilca. Your father's debt is paid. All honor flows to him from this time forth. But tell me this one thing, are you a man or a maid?"

Mizilca smiled and did not answer, just turned the horse's head to the gate and rode away. But once she was through the gate, she turned around and opened her shirt, so that there was left no doubt in the Sultan's mind that she was indeed a young woman . . . and beautiful.

"A maid has served thee one full year and yet ye did not know her," she called back.

Then, spurring her horse, Mizilca rode home to a great feast and much laughter. Her father and all his company revered and respected Mizilca from that day forth.

POLAND/JEWISH

The Pirate Princess

*Sometimes a young woman has
to make her own fate*

ONCE, LONG AGO, in two faraway kingdoms, there were two kings who were both childless.

They each so needed an heir that they set out on long journeys seeking remedies. The one went east, the other west, but as God willed it, they met at the same place, on the same day, at the same time.

The place was a sorcerer's cave, and since neither king would let the other go first, they entered together.

"What is it you will?" asked the sorcerer.

"A child!" they said together.

The sorcerer, a hawk-faced man in a dirty turban, put his finger to the side of his nose. "Ah," he said. "I have read of these children in the stars. One a boy, one a girl. As such they are destined to marry, even as you were destined to come to my cave on the same day and at the same time. If you permit them to marry, you and your descendants will share a great blessing."

"Ah," the two kings said together.

"But if for any reason you keep them apart," the sorcerer warned, "many will suffer the consequences."

"I give my hand on it," said the one king.

"And I," said the other. They clasped hands like old friends.

The sorcerer put his own hands on theirs. "The betrothal is complete."

NOW, IT HAPPENED THAT before a year was out, both kings had become fathers, one to a handsome boy and the other to a lovely girl. Such was their joy that in each kingdom a year of feasting and rejoicing was proclaimed.

But one kingdom was far to the east and one far to the west. There are many years between a birth and a wedding, and many decisions and rulings and pacts and battles during that time. The two kings were so distracted by the day-to-day problems of running a kingdom that neither of them remembered the vow made in the sorcerer's cave. Or if they did, they remembered it as if it had been a dream.

When the young prince and the young princess came of age, their fathers sent them off to study in a foreign land known for the wisdom of its scholars. And the same fate that had guided their fathers to the cave brought them to the same town and to the same school and to the same teacher. And it will not come as a surprise that their teacher was none other than the sorcerer from the cave.

Over the course of their years of study, the prince and princess fell in love and vowed to wed. But they told no one of their vows, not even their teacher. If he guessed, he did not say.

At last the years of study were over and the prince and princess had to be parted—the one to go home to the east, the other to go home to the west.

APART FROM HIS BELOVED, the prince had fallen to sighing. He stopped eating. He stayed day and night in an unlit room.

Worried that his son was dying of some unnamed illness, the prince's father went to see him, accompanied by physicians. "What is wrong?" asked the king.

"I am in love," said the prince.

Fearing his son had taken up with some unsuitable girl, the king sent away the physicians and sat on his son's bed. "Tell me who she is."

But when he heard the girl's name, the king broke into a great smile. He recognized that she was the daughter of the king whose hand he had taken so many years ago. Quickly he retold the story of that meeting to the prince. "Do not fear. Rise up and eat, my son. I shall write to your princess's father, reminding him of the vow we made; you shall hand it to him yourself, and all will be well."

NOW, THE PRINCESS, too, had been failing since the two had parted. But she had not told her father what was wrong. When the young prince arrived with the letter from his father, the king grew afraid.

He had, in fact, forgotten entirely about the vow made in the cave. While his daughter had been away studying in a foreign land, he had—all unbeknownst to her—given pledge of her marriage to the son of the rich and powerful king whose lands bordered his own.

What could he do? If he broke that marriage pledge, his lands would be forfeit to his neighbor. But if he broke the sorcerer's vow, many would suffer the consequences.

So, not knowing what to do, he dithered and dallied and delayed as long as possible, neither letting the young prince see the princess nor telling her that her true love was at court.

So, there they were—apart and yet close together for many days.

NOW, ONE DAY the princess overheard two servants whispering about the prince, and she heard in which room her father had put him. She managed to stroll by the room until he caught sight of her in the mirror. After that they managed to meet secretly in the garden, where the princess told him that her father had betrothed her to another.

"Then we must run away," the prince said to her, pulling an apple from the tree. He took a knife and sliced the apple in two. Then, giving her one half, he himself took the other. They ate the two halves and kissed, their breaths sweetened with the apple. Then the princess pledged that what was once whole would be whole again.

That very night they climbed out of their chamber windows and met again under the apple tree in the garden. From there they fled over the wall and through the town and down to the shore, where a small ship bobbed in the harbor.

The prince pulled up the anchor, and off they went, out of the harbor and onto the great wide sea.

By the time it had been discovered that they were gone, they were already far away. And though the king wept and wailed and tore at his beard, what could he do?

THE PRINCE AND PRINCESS sailed on and on until they were in need of provisions, for the ship had but a small larder. So when the prince spied an island, they put in to shore, where they saw all manner of fruit growing, but high up in the smallest branches of the trees.

It was too dangerous for the prince, who was the heavier, to climb those trees. So the princess tucked her skirts into her waistband and climbed instead, high up to the small branches of a date palm, where she tossed down fruit after fruit to the prince, who waited below with a sack.

And all would have been well, but destiny was not done with them yet.

A merchant ship was passing by, and the merchant's son, standing on the deck with a spyglass, saw the princess in the palm tree, her long slim legs wrapped around the trunk, her dark hair falling loose around her face.

It was as if his heart had been pierced with an arrow, so swiftly did he fall in love.

"Row me to shore," he instructed his men. And they climbed into the rowboat and headed toward the island.

Now, from her vantage in the tree, the princess saw the boat with the merchant's son and seven armed men coming ashore. So, she called down to the prince, "Hide, my love. Do not reveal yourself, whatever happens. These men will not hurt me, but they might very well kill you. And if you die, I shall die, too."

Then she tossed down her ring to him, saying, "This is my pledge to you forever."

The prince hid himself in the dense wood, for though he was brave, he was not foolhardy, and one unarmed against so many would have had no chance at all. Still, the princess would not climb down from the tree.

The boat came to the shore, and the merchant's son led his men to the tree, and they encircled it.

"Come down, sweet maid," the merchant's son said, "for I have fallen in love with you and would have you be mine."

The princess did not move.

The merchant's son talked sweetly, then he talked quickly, then he talked angrily, and then—without any more talking—he had his men cut down the tree, and the princess was forced to go with him to his ship.

"Tell me your name, fair one," he said.

"I will not tell you that, or the country I come from, unless you vow not to touch me until we are married. And once that is done, I will tell you all," the princess said.

So smitten was the merchant's son that he agreed.

THE MERCHANT'S BOAT sailed away, leaving the hidden prince behind. And while the princess sang to the merchant's son and entertained him on a lyre that he had in his cabin, she would not let him touch even her hand.

"For you must be mindful of your vow," she said.

If she thought that by denying him he would become bored with her, she was wrong. He fell still more deeply in love.

THE DAY CAME AT LAST when the merchant's boat sailed into its home port. The holds of the ship were stuffed with valuable cargo.

"You go ashore, my husband-to-be," the princess said. "Tell your family what it is you bring them. For it would not be polite or wise to simply show up at the door with me on your arm."

The merchant's son saw the wisdom in what she said.

"And let the sailors drink a glass of wine in my honor as well," said the princess.

To this, too, he agreed.

But no sooner had the merchant's son left the ship than the princess made certain that the sailors had more than one glass of wine. In fact, she opened an entire barrel for them. And soon the sailors were all drunk and wanting to go into town for pleasure.

The princess gladly gave them leave, and off they went.

No sooner had they all left the ship than the princess hauled up the anchor, unfurled the sails, and sailed out of the harbor on a steady breeze.

WHEN THE MERCHANT'S SON returned with his family to greet his prospective bride, the ship was gone, and onshore the drunken sailors stumbled around, unsteady and uncertain.

The merchant was furious, for they had not only lost the bride-to-be but the ship and all it carried. Taking his cane, the merchant hit his son on the head and the shoulders, shouting, "Better in the hand than in the heart! Stupid boy, go from my sight."

So the merchant's son was driven from his home to become a lonely wanderer. The princess had set sail in a great ship by herself. The prince was abandoned on an island. And the two kings did not know where their children were.

NOW, AS THE PRINCESS sailed by one kingdom, the ruler of that country was in his palace on the shore and, as usual, was looking out with a telescope at the passing boats. When he saw the princess's ship, it seemed to have no sailors on board, and so he sent his fleet to capture it.

When the ship was brought into the harbor and the princess escorted down the plank, the king was so struck by her beauty and her bearing that he knew her for royalty.

"Will you be my bride?" he asked, without more preamble than that.

The princess looked at him and nodded once. "On three conditions, Your Majesty," she said.

"And what, fair maid, are they?" he answered.

"You will not touch me until after the wedding."

"Agreed," said the king.

"You will not allow my ship to be unloaded until that time, for I would not want you or your advisors to see what prizes I have brought as my dowry."

"Agreed," said the king.

"And I would have eleven maidens as my ladies-in-waiting."

Since none of this seemed more than he could give, the king nodded. "Agreed again."

The wedding plans were made, and a lavish wedding it was to be, indeed. Eleven daughters of the highest lords of the land were chosen as the bride-to-be's ladies. There was great joy in the kingdom.

But at dusk, the day before the marriage vows were to be spoken, the princess turned to her eleven ladies.

"Come and see my ship, which no one else has seen," she said.

As not a one of them had ever set foot on a ship before, they all went eagerly down to the harbor, which was lovely against the darkening sky. Eagerly they looked at the cabins and the hammocks and the clever little cupboards in the ship. And eagerly they drank the wine the princess served them.

"To the king's health!" she called gaily, and they toasted him again.

And again.

And again.

Then one by one, made dozy by the drinking, the maidens all fell to sleep. All—except for the princess.

When all were *fast* asleep, the princess untied the moorings, hoisted the sails, and off went the ship down the swift sea-lanes.

Now, someone reported to the king that the princess's ship was gone, and, worried that she would fret over the loss of her dowry, the king went to tell her.

She was not in her chamber.

She was not in her hall.

And she was not with her ladies-in-waiting. In fact, he could not find the ladies-in-waiting, either.

It finally dawned on him—though it was not before dawn itself—that the princess and her eleven ladies were gone with the ship.

When the news got out, the eleven great lords of the land were so enraged at the loss of their daughters that the king was forced to give up his throne and become a wanderer in the land.

IT WAS MIDMORNING when the eleven ladies awoke and found themselves far out at sea, with no land in sight. What a weeping and a wailing there was then. All of them crying and carrying on. All, that is, but the princess.

"Well, we are here, and we will make the best of it," she said, and she taught them to sew up their dresses into trousers and take off their heavy corsets and wear their bodices like shirts.

So they continued on the ship, riding the currents of wind and wave, getting better at sailing each day, until they were sailors as good as the men who had brought the ship to shore. And they kept the ship tidy, besides.

At last, with the stores running low, they came to an island—not the island on which the prince had been left but another island.

"Here we will find fresh fruit and water," said the princess.

So they trimmed their sails and in they went, into a sweet little harbor that nestled on the east side of the island.

Though the prince was not there, a pirate crew was, having landed on the west side of the island. They saw the ladies, and at first thinking them king's sailors, advanced with drawn weapons. But soon they realized their mistake.

"Come with us!" they said. And around the island to the other side went the princess and her eleven ladies-in-waiting, forced at sword's point to do what the captors proposed.

When they arrived at the pirates' camp, the princess stepped up boldly to the chief. "We, too, are pirates," she said. "And while you use force— we use our wits."

The pirates began to growl and make noises that were both rude and frightening. But the princess refused to be frightened. And her very refusal to show fear put heart in her ladies.

The pirate captain looked at her with growing interest. "Speak on," he said.

"There are twelve of us and twelve of you. And if you were wise, you would take us each to wife and make use of our wisdom. For our part, we will each contribute a twelfth part of our wealth as our dowries."

Now, the captain—who was captain because he, above all others, did have some wit—had already fallen in love with the princess. He was delighted to hear her proposal. And so he instructed his men to go on board the princess's ship with the ladies-in-waiting.

There they admired the wealth and the tidy ship and drank toasts in wine—to the captain, to the princess, to the ladies one at a time. And at last, exhausted by their merrymaking, they fell asleep, slobbering and snoring.

As soon as she was certain the pirates were well and truly out cold, the princess called her ladies to her. "Now we must each of us kill her man. I shall do the pirate chief, and you must do the rest."

They slaughtered the drunken louts with their own swords and tossed them overboard, then went back to see what riches the pirates had in store.

It was the greatest treasure any of them had ever seen—bejeweled cups and great strings of pearls, gold by the bowlful, and precious gems as big as hens' eggs. There was scarce room for it all on the ship, and much they had to leave behind.

SO, ONCE AGAIN they went off to sea, but this time they came at last to a great harbor. With their roughened hands and reddened faces, and in their tattered makeshift trousers, they were taken for men.

Delighted to be onshore, they went into the center of the city, and it was the largest city any of them had ever seen. But there was a great hubbub and a hullabaloo in the city, and they saw thousands of people running to and fro, seemingly without reason.

"What has happened?" asked one of the lady sailors.

"Oh sir, you are clearly not from here," said a young ribbon seller. "The queen is about to choose a new king."

"What has happened to the old one?" asked another of the lady sailors, careful to keep her voice low.

"He has died," said a button seller.

"That is too bad," said a third. "Did he have sons?"

"None," said an alewife. "So now, according to our custom, the queen will go to the roof of the palace and throw down the crown. And whoever's head it lands on—that person will be our new king."

"So that is why the hubbub," said the fourth lady sailor.

"Everyone trying to be the new king!" said the fifth.

But the princess was at the end of the line of sailors and did not hear this explanation, and when a heavy object fell on her head, she only cried out, "Oh my!"

Immediately at her side were a vizier and three great wise men of the kingdom, crying out, "Long live our king!" for they did not realize she was a woman.

THE PRINCESS DID NOT tell them. She was too wise for that. But when the funeral of the old king was over, a wedding was to take place between the princess-disguised-as-a-man and the old king's widow.

"This sailor is too young for the old queen," said the vizier, noting the beardless chin of the sailor. "It will not be a good marriage. What children could come of it?"

For a moment the princess was relieved. Only a moment.

"Let us marry him to the queen's daughter instead."

And the old queen, tired of ruling, thought it a fine idea. "But let it happen at once," she said.

So, the wedding was set for the very next day.

But the disguised princess shook her head. "I am just newly come to this city. I have been traveling on the sea too many days. Let me grow used to your ways, and let me clothe my men in silken trousers and linen shirts, and let our hands grow less rough and our faces less red from the sun and the sea."

This was so wise that the vizier agreed.

"And furthermore," said the disguised princess, "let many sculptures of my head be made and set at every crossroads and every road leading to and from this great city, that my people will get to know me."

And that, too, seemed wise, and so the vizier agreed.

"But anyone who stops and shows great emotion at the sculpture—arrest them and bring them to me, for surely that will bode ill for this kingdom."

And that, too, seemed wise, and so, for a third time, the vizier agreed.

NOW, IT HAPPENED that three people—and only three—stopped and gawked at the stone heads with such obvious emotion that they were arrested at once.

The first was the true bridegroom, who had made his way from the island.

The second was the merchant's son, sent off by his angry father.

And the third was the king who had been banished by the eleven lords.

Each had recognized in the new king's stone head the princess's lovely face.

On the very day of the wedding, the princess-in-disguise had these three brought to her, and she asked them to tell their stories. And when these were told, she turned first to the king.

"O King, your kingdom was lost because these ladies were lost. Take them back and you will surely be welcomed." She gestured to her ladies-in-waiting, no longer dressed as men—and who, with soft hands and tanned cheeks, glowed with beauty.

And to the merchant's son she said, "And you who were driven from your home because of lost wealth, take back your ship, which carries a greater wealth than before, and surely your father will welcome you."

And then at last she turned to the prince. "It is you I have loved forever. It is you I will marry."

She called the vizier and the three wise men to her, saying, "I am not a man who stands before you but a woman and a princess." She showed them the ring, which the prince had kept with him always. "Before I was ever a man, I was to be married to this man. Nothing shall part us now."

The vizier and the wise men were astonished. "But you are our king, what shall we do?"

The princess had an answer. "Let the queen's daughter be married to the king and sail off with him and the eleven ladies. Let the merchant's son provide a handsome dowry."

"And who shall rule here?" the vizier asked.

"Why, we shall," said the princess, holding tight to the prince's hand.

So, the princess and the prince married and reigned with mercy and justice till the day they died.

JAPAN

The Samurai Maiden

Sacrifice or hero—this maiden has a choice

ONCE, LONG AGO, in the island nation of Japan—which sits like a string of pearls stretched out along the ocean—a great samurai lord, Oribe Shima, was banished by the emperor for some small slight. He was sent to the wild and rocky islets called the Oki Islands, leaving behind his beloved small daughter, Tokoyo, in the care of her nurse.

They were separated for many years, and Tokoyo felt the pain and humiliation as much as her father. So, one day, when she was almost all grown, she decided that she would try to find him.

"And if I die trying," she told her nurse, "then at least it will be an honorable death." Which is what one would expect to hear from a great samurai lord's child. She had inherited her father's spirit, and she kept herself fit by diving with the local pearl divers—women whose job it was to collect the pearl oysters from the bottom of the sea.

Selling all that she had, Tokoyo set out for Akasaki, where, on days as bright as pearls, she could see the rocky coasts where her father had been abandoned.

No one in Akasaki would take her across the sea to the Oki Islands, for the sea was hard to cross. Besides, there was a law forbidding anyone to visit those banished. To break that law meant death.

But Tokoyo would not give up. She bought a small boat and some food. Then, in the dark of night, she set sail all alone.

Fortune could have turned a back on Tokoyo but did not. A light breeze and a strong current carried her across the rough sea, and she fetched up—half dead and chilled to the bone—on the nearest of the rocky islets. She crawled out of the boat, dragged it ashore, then found a sheltered spot, where she slept until dawn.

When she awoke she began her search and, before long, came upon a fisherman.

"I am the daughter of Oribe Shima," she said, "the great samurai lord. Do you know him?"

"Alas—I do not," said the fisherman. "But do not ask me more. Such questions may bring you to your death. And me to mine."

Tokoyo bowed and went on. But so fearful was she of bringing death to someone else—though she did not fear it for herself—she did not dare ask further. Soon her food ran out and she was forced to beg from strangers. Still, she did it with grace and with the hope that she would find her father one day.

Now, one evening she came to a shrine, which stood on the very edge of a rocky ledge.

I will pray here to the Buddha, she thought, *and ask him for help. For if I can ask no one else, at least Buddha will listen.* But her prayers were so long and so anguished, she was drained when she finished, and she fell asleep right there at the shrine.

In the middle of the night, she was awakened by the sound of anguished weeping and a clapping of hands. Sitting up, she looked around and saw by the moonlight a girl and a priest, both dressed in flowing white robes.

It was the priest who was clapping and the girl who was sobbing. And when the priest stopped clapping, he took the girl by the shoulder and led her to the very edge of the precipice. It was quite clear that he was about to push her over the edge.

Tokoyo leaped up, ran over to the pair, and grabbed the girl just before she went over the side of the cliff.

The priest sighed. "I judge from your actions that you are a stranger to our island, for if you knew what we do here, you would not be so rash in your rescue."

"What can excuse such a thing?" Tokoyo asked, her arms around the sobbing girl.

"This island is cursed by the evil serpent Yofune-Nushi. He lives below this cliff at the bottom of the sea. Every year he demands that we throw a girl not yet fifteen years old into the sea on this day. If we do not send him a sacrifice, he causes great storms at sea and many of our fishermen drown. So we give one to save all."

Tokoyo listened to what he had to say. Then she spoke with great deliberation. "Holy monk, let this child go, and I shall take her place. I am the daughter of the great samurai warrior chief Oribe Shima, exiled to these islands. I cannot find him. I cannot even ask about him. But I will do as he would have done. Since I cannot live a happy life, let me die a death of sacrifice. All I ask is that, if you can, you deliver this letter to my father, whose name you may not even be allowed to speak."

Tokoyo took the girl's white robe and put it on. Then she knelt again at the shrine. "Buddha," she pleaded, "give me my father's courage," for she did not plan to go quietly into the sea but intended to try to defeat the serpent god so that no more girls would have to be given into his wicked coils.

Upon rising she took from her waistband the last thing of worth that she had taken from her house, a dagger that had belonged to her father and his fathers before him. Holding it in her teeth the way the pearl divers had taught her, she dived into the sea.

Down and down and down Tokoyo dived, slicing cleanly through the water. When she reached the bottom, there in front of her was a cave all aglitter with shells.

When Tokoyo peered into the cave, she thought she saw a man sitting a little ways inside. Grasping her father's dagger she went in. But there was no man there. What she had mistakenly taken for one was a statue of the emperor who had exiled her father.

Angrily she raised her knife. If she could not strike the emperor himself, she could at least deface his statue.

Then suddenly she felt flooded with forgiveness.

I will return evil with good, she thought, and clenched the knife once again in her teeth.

She undid the sash of the white robe and tied the statue to her back. Then she headed with powerful strokes out of the cave.

What should greet her at the cave's entrance but a great, horrible snakelike creature with glowing scales and a hundred tiny feet. Its mouth was open and its teeth glittered as if coated with phosphorescence.

She knew at once it was Yofune-Nushi.

Without thinking about the danger, Tokoyo swam up close to his dreadful face and with one stroke of the knife put out his right eye.

Yofune-Nushi twisted and turned in his agony, spinning Tokoyo and her heavy burden around. At last Tokoyo managed to pull the knife from the creature's eye.

Yofune-Nushi tried to get to the safety of his cave, though blinded in the one eye, and he could not find the way. So he turned, wallowing in front of the entrance, and Tokoyo struck him in the heart.

Then, with her last bit of breath, she tied the end of the sash around the dead monster's neck and towed him up to the surface of the ocean.

Imagine the astonishment of the priest and the girl, who, standing on the cliff side and watching the great lashings of waves, saw Tokoyo rise up with a wooden statue tied to her back and the defeated evil serpent dragging behind. They rushed down to the beach and helped her to shore.

Then, while the priest stood watch as the exhausted Tokoyo slept, the girl raced back to the village and told the news.

What a festival began then! The emperor's statue and the great head of the serpent god were brought into town. And Tokoyo herself was borne to the town center on a litter. There were seven days of singing and dancing and celebration. Word went to the emperor himself of Tokoyo's amazing feat of courage and strength.

The emperor, who had long suffered from a strange malady, suddenly found himself cured.

"That is because your statue had been cursed and sunk in the sea," said his advisors. "This brave girl has not only saved the village, she has saved the emperor's life."

"And what is the name of this girl?" the emperor asked.

"Tokoyo," said the advisors.

"Daughter of Oribe Shima," they added.

"Oribe Shima," the emperor said, musing. "For his daughter's brave deed, let him be released from banishment. Let him come home."

When it was discovered that Oribe Shima's lands had been taken from him, and that Tokoyo had been forced to sell what little was left, all was returned—and twice that, as well. So Tokoyo and her father were reunited. They found where her old nurse had gone and brought her back to live with them. And they dwelt happily together again for as long as they all lived.

FRANCE

Bradamante

*A great medieval knight in shining armor—
and she's a woman!*

ONCE, IN THE TIME of the great emperor Charlemagne, there was a vassal king Agramant, who had many brave knights. Among the bravest was Bradamante, the knight of the white plume and shield. Bradamante was strong in arm, fierce in heart, and true to both king and crown. Bradamante's story is told in many parts. Here are two of them.

IN THE MIDST of a great battle, in which Bradamante was fighting with determination against a Moorish enemy named Rodomonte, the troops of Charlemagne were suddenly put to flight. But neither Bradamante nor Rodomonte noticed that the field had been cleared, for they traded blow upon blow without ceasing.

Seeing that all the rest of the Christian army had fled, a Moorish prince named Ruggiero interrupted the fight, saying, "Let him of the two who worships Christ pause and hear what I have to say. The army of Charles is routed, and if he wishes to follow his leader, he has no time for delay."

Bradamante was thunderstruck by the loss. "Gladly I go, and I thank you, gentle prince, for your honor." Then, wheeling about, horse and rider raced off the field.

But this was not Rodomonte's choice. He cried after the departing Bradamante, "Coward—come back! I do not consent that you leave!"

"That brave knight's leaving was no cowardly act. But if you must pursue the fight," said the prince, "I will take that brave knight's part against you, though we be on the same side." And he gave Rodomonte such a blow to the head that the man dropped both his sword and bridle.

Then Ruggiero sat back, waiting for Rodomonte to recover his wits.

Just then Bradamante, looking back, saw what was happening and returned. "I cannot let you fight my battle for me, O honorable prince."

But the battle was, in fact, over. Rodomonte, recovering from his confusion, picked up his sword, remounted his horse, and galloped out of sight.

And so Bradamante and Ruggiero, who should have been enemies, became friends and rode from the battlefield together.

Ruggiero spoke of how his mother, a daughter of the house of Hector of Troy, had been driven from her home in Messina and had died giving him birth. "And so I was brought up and trained to arms by a sage sorcerer."

"I am of the race of Clermont," Bradamante said. "Perhaps you have heard of my brother, Rinaldo."

"I have heard of him, indeed," said the prince. "But not that he had a brother."

"He has no brother, indeed," said Bradamante. "For I am his sister." She took off her helmet, and she was so lovely to look at, the prince was transported with delight.

As they rode along, they were so intent on their conversation that neither of them paid attention to what was going on around them. A party of Moors—waiting in the woods to intercept any fleeing Christians—broke from its ambush.

"After them!" shouted one soldier, who rushed upon the pair and gave

Bradamante such a blow upon her uncasqued head that blood flowed freely, like red tresses, down into her hair.

But Bradamante was not deterred by the blow. She put her helmet back on, and with Ruggiero by her side, she chased the ambushers back into the forest.

During the chase Bradamante and the Moorish prince became separated, and they, who had so recently found each other, were lost.

LONG DID BRADAMANTE look for the handsome prince Ruggiero, but it was as if he had disappeared from the face of the earth. She left Charlemagne's army and the vassalage of King Agramant in order to continue her search.

And then one day she found herself in a broad meadow surrounded by the steepest of mountain ravines. In the middle of the meadow was a stone fountain. Ancient trees overshadowed the fountain, and Bradamante—hot and tired from traveling so far and so high—decided that it was the perfect Eden in which to rest.

When she got nearer the place, she saw that there was a knight sitting with his back against one of the trees, and he seemed in the deepest of griefs. So she dismounted and went over to him, asking, "What ails you, pale knight?"

"Alas, my lord," he said, for in her battle dress he mistook her for a man, "the young woman I am to marry has been ripped from me by a demon enchanter on a winged horse. Though I have followed them as fast as I could, over the rocks and through the ravines till I killed the horse under me, I can now only lie here, awaiting my own death, for I can go no farther."

"Come, come, surely more can be done," said Bradamante, for though she sorrowed for the fate of the maiden torn from him, she could not abide one who would so easily will himself to die.

"And more I have done," said the knight, sighing. "I have sent already two good men after her, braver and stronger by far than I—the king of Sericane, Gradassso, and the Moorish prince Ruggiero. But the wicked enchanter has captured them both and taken them to his castle, high in these mountains. It is a place that no mortal man can break into."

At the mention of Ruggiero's name, Bradamante thought her heart would burst through her armor, but she did not let it show. Instead she said, "Do not despair, sir knight. This day may end more happily than you think. Show me to this impregnable castle. What one cannot do, perhaps another can."

Encouraged by Bradamante's enthusiasm, the young knight stood. He followed the lady knight across the meadow, and they started up the steep side of a ravine. Just then they were overtaken by a messenger from King Agramant's camp who cried out, "My lady, Bradamante! His Majesty commands you to return to the army."

"I will not return till I have helped this young man rescue his beloved, and rescued two brave men besides," Bradamante told the messenger. As she spoke to the messenger, she had her back to the young knight and did not see the look on his face.

Bradamante! he was thinking. *Of all the knights to find me here . . .* For he was Sir Pinabel of the house of Mayence, which had long been feuding with Bradamante's own house of Clermont. "If I do not rid myself of her, she will surely do me mortal injury." And he resolved not to tell her his name or his lineage but to find some way to slay her surreptitiously. He knew he could not hope to kill her in a fair fight.

Bradamante knew none of this, of course, and she encouraged the young man, saying, "We shall together find a way to bring your fair maiden home. Do not fear. Do not lose heart."

As they proceeded up the trail, leading their horses, Pinabel no longer thought of his bride-to-be. All he could think of was how to get rid of the lady knight. So he proposed that he go ahead a little ways up the ravine.

"Thus I may scout out our whereabouts and see if there is shelter for the night," said Pinabel.

"I am pleased," said Bradamante to him, "that you have given up simply waiting for death, for it will come upon us all in time without our greeting it."

She did not see the sneer on his face as he left.

Pinabel soon found a cleft in the rock and, looking down through it, discovered that it widened below into a spacious cavern. Meanwhile Bradamante, after scouting on either side for enemies and finding none, hurried after him.

"See that cavern?" Pinabel asked. "I just saw a beautiful damsel there who was weeping and crying out for help. I was just about to make my way to her when a ruffian came from behind and dragged her away."

"It is too far to jump with safety," declared Bradamante. She looked around and found a large elm growing out of the side of the ravine. Lopping off one mighty branch of it, she thrust it into the opening. "There," she said, "I have made a bridge. You hold tight one end and I will climb down. Then I will hold the bottom and you can come after me."

So it was agreed. But as she started down the branch, Pinabel called out, "Are you a good leaper?" and let go of his end of the branch so that branch and Bradamante fell into the pit. Then he ran off, back down the ravine.

But if he thought to murder her, Pinabel was mistaken. The foliage cushioned her fall and she was not seriously injured, though for a long moment she was stunned and could not move.

At last able to stand again, Bradamante saw that the cavern was not a natural place at all. There was a door at one end and a torch flickering in a holder beside it.

Grasping the torch, she examined the door and saw that there was a simple latch. She opened the door and passed into another cavern, loftier than the first, which looked like some kind of temple, for there were alabaster columns supporting an alabaster roof. In the middle of this chamber was a simple altar, over which hung a lamp, the radiance of which was reflected back by the alabaster so that the entire room shimmered with rainbows.

Bradamante fell to her knees in awe and prayed aloud. "I thank Thee for preserving me." She heard the sound of a door opening, looked up, and saw a woman coming toward her with flowing robes.

"Brave and gracious Bradamante, arise," the woman said.

"You know my name?" Bradamante was puzzled.

"Not I but my master, the spirit of Merlin, whose last earthly abode was this place. He answers questions of those who approach his tomb."

"Who am I," Bradamante said modestly, "that the great Merlin himself should speak to me?" Still, she held a secret satisfaction that it was so, and so she followed the maiden to the altar.

No sooner had they come close to the altar than a voice filled the cavern, saying, "O noble maiden, future mother of heroes, great captains and renowned knights shall be numbered among your descendants."

"Whom . . ." She breathed the word. "Whom shall I marry?"

"Ruggiero shall be your bridegroom. Fly then to his deliverance, and lay in the dust the wicked enchanter who has snatched him from you and holds him in chains."

It was what she wanted to hear. "But I do not know the way," she reminded Merlin's voice.

"I know the way," said the woman. "Tomorrow morning we will climb through the mountain's hidden passageways and I will lead you there."

THE NEXT MORNING, good as her word, the young woman led Bradamante between rocks and precipices, and across rapid rivers, imparting to the lady knight much important knowledge as they went.

"The enchanter's castle is indeed impenetrable by normal means," she said. "And his winged steed is a hippogriff, with the head of an eagle—and claws and talons—but the body of a horse. Even more, the enchanter bears a magic buckler, which flashes a light so brilliant, anyone who looks at it is struck blind. Yet, you cannot just close your eyes against it, for how then would you fight him?"

"How indeed," Bradamante remarked. "With no magic of my own."

"Ah, but magic you shall have. For the king of the Moors also desires to rescue young Ruggiero, whom he loves like a son. He has a magic ring that renders all other enchantments useless and he has given it to his craftiest servant, the dwarf Brunello. If you can get the ring from this creature, then you—and not Brunello—will have a chance to set Ruggiero free."

They made one more torturous turn through the mountainside and, to Bradamante's astonishment, came out into a clearing. In front of them was a rich and wide river pouring out into the sea.

"Not far from here, in the city of Bordeaux, is a hostelry called the Spotted Hound," the woman said. "There you will find the Moor's dwarf, and you will recognize him because he is but four feet tall, with thick eyebrows and a tufted beard. You can tell him that you are a knight seeking to combat the enchanter, but do not let him know that you know about the ring."

"I see," said Bradamante, though she was not sure she understood anything at all.

"Let him offer to be your guide, and you offer to be his sword. But take care to stay behind him till you see the castle before you. Then do not hesitate—strike him dead, for the wretch deserves no pity from you. However, do not let him suspect you, for he will put the ring in his mouth and become invisible at once."

So saying, the young woman took her leave of Bradamante, and the lady knight was on her own.

ALL WENT AS Merlin's young acolyte predicted. Bradamante had no trouble discovering the dwarf, and even less trouble engaging him in conversation. She did not ever say her true name or her sex, not her religion or the country she came from. And as they sat outside speaking—for the day was warm—there was a sudden shout from the people around them.

Bradamante stood and looked where the people pointed, and in the sky was a winged horse with feathers all colors of the rainbow. A mounted knight sat on the horse's back, and in moments steed and rider disappeared behind the summits of the mountains.

"It is the enchanter I seek," said the dwarf.

"I, too," said Bradamante, "though I know not how to go after him."

"Why, I have a map," said the dwarf. "If you lend me your sword and right hand to keep me safe from wild animals and wilder men, I shall guide you there."

They shook hands on it then and there. And the next morning, having purchased two horses for their trip, off they went into the Pyrenees, and by a route very different from the one Bradamante had taken with Pinabel, to the very summit of the mountains where one can look down at Spain, France, and the two seas.

IT TOOK A day and a night and a day before they got there and, from the top, made their way, by a fatiguing ride, into a deep valley. But eventually they found themselves before an isolated mountain upon the summit of which stood a castle hewn out of the rock, surrounded with a wall of brass.

"There is the enchanter's castle," said Brunello. "One must have wings to mount to that place." He got off his horse and stood marveling at it. Bradamante got off her horse as well, standing a bit behind the dwarf.

Seeing the castle she knew that the time had come for her to take the magic ring, but she could not in good faith slay an unarmed man. So she seized him before he was aware of what she was up to, tied him to a tree, and skinned the ring from his finger.

"What are you doing? You do not know what you do!" he shouted. "You do not know who I am!"

But Bradamante did not listen. Instead she got back on her horse, advanced to the foot of the castle rock, and took her battle horn from her belt. She blew her challenge into it loud and long.

Suddenly from the top of the castle's turrets, rising to her call, flew the enchanter on his winged horse. Three times he circled around her before landing in front of her.

Bradamante was relieved to see he bore no lance or club. He had only, on his arm, the dreaded buckler and, in his hand, an open book.

Bradamante drew her sword and struck first one side and then the other, but all she wounded was the wind. Then, slicing three more times, she dismounted to appear as if she planned to continue the battle on foot.

The enchanter uncovered the magic buckler, but when he held it high—because Bradamante had the ring that confounded all magic—it did not blind her. However, the enchanter did not know this, and when she threw herself down on the ground, pretending to be overcome by the shield, he dismounted and, with a set of chains to bind her, approached her.

Bradamante waited until he was near and then she sprang up, seized him, threw him down, and with his own chains bound him fast.

"Take my life, as you take my magic, young man!" he cried.

But Bradamante did no such thing.

"Tell me first your name and why you have built this fortress. And tell me, too, why you have captured all these fine knights and maidens."

"Alas," cried the magician, tears spilling down his face, "I built this castle only to guard the life of the young knight I raised from birth. My arts showed me that he was to become a Christian and after that perish by the blackest of treasons."

"And the youth's name?" whispered Bradamante, unable to speak aloud.

"Ruggiero," the enchanter said. "And I am the unhappy Atlante, who has reared him from childhood. He went from me to serve his king, but fearing for his life I have conspired to bring him back. I have collected a great many young knights and ladies to render his captivity light, for they can amuse him and keep his thoughts from battles and glory."

"But if those are the things he wishes for—" Bradamante said.

"You young men are all alike." The magician sighed. "Yet I beg you— take my magical steed and my buckler. Take what friends of yours are up in my castle. Only take me back there and leave me with my glorious son. Or else kill me on the spot!"

"It is Ruggiero alone I seek," said Bradamante. "Your entreaties are in vain, old man. You wish to keep him here in a life of sloth and pleasure, fearing that which your magic foresees. Foolish father! You could not even foresee your own fortune. Nor guess my secret."

She took off her battle helmet. "My name is Bradamante and I am called the lady knight. Take me up on your steed and loose all the prisoners. I shall not kill you. Ruggiero's father is my father, too."

Then they rode up to the castle and all the prisoners were freed— though some, it must be said, regretted leaving.

As for Ruggiero, when he saw Bradamante, he was rapturous with joy. They pledged their love. And if they did not live happily ever after, it was because they had many more adventures to come.

ENGLAND

Molly Whuppie

Smart, forward, and brave—
that's the very definition of a hero

ONCE UPON A TIME there were a man and a wife who had one-two-three-four-five—too many children, and they could not feed them all. So, they took the three youngest and left them in the deepest part of a dark and tangled wood.

Hand in hand in hand, the three little girls walked and walked, looking for a way home, but they could find none. They just got more lost and more frightened and more hungry.

At last they were so deep in the woods, they had all but given themselves up to despair, when they spied a light.

"Look," said the youngest, whose name was Molly Whuppie, "there is a house. We can stop there for the night, and get something to eat besides." Oh, that Molly Whuppie was a smart girl!

So, they rapped on the door, and a woman came out who was as broad as she was tall. "What do ye want?" asked the woman.

"Please, ma'am," said Molly, "let us in and give us some bread." Oh, that Molly Whuppie was a forward girl!

"That I dare not do," said the woman, "for my husband is a giant and he would as soon kill ye as look at ye."

"Then let us stop for a while," begged Molly. "We will be away before he comes home." Oh, that Molly Whuppie was a brave girl!

So the woman took them in and she had just set them down by the fire with some milk and bread when there came a great knock at the door.

"Fe-fi-fo-fum," said the voice.

"Oh dear," said the woman, "it is my husband himself. Do not say a word."

And into the house came the giant. He was ten feet tall and his head scraped the rooftree. His hands were like shovels. His teeth like knives.

"Fe-fi-fo-fum, I smell the blood of some earthly one," said the giant. "Who's here, wife?"

"Just three small lassies," said the giant's wife. "They are hungry and cold. And not a bite between them. So ye leave them be." She shook her wooden spoon at him.

So he sat down at the table, ignoring the girls, and ate an entire cow at one sitting. *Whooomp!* Just like that. And when he was done, he turned in his chair and stared at the three girls—the two who shook in their boots, and little Molly Whuppie.

"I have three lassies of my own," he said in that great awful voice. "They will like some company. So ye shall sleep this night with them." And he led them up a wooden ladder to a loft, where the giant's lassies lay tucked into bed, snoring through their slit nostrils and whistling through their fangs.

The oldest of the girls relaxed then. "He's not so bad after all," she whispered to Molly Whuppie as they all climbed into the giant bed. And soon enough they were fast asleep. All except Molly Whuppie, though she pretended to be.

Then the giant returned, and he placed straw ropes around Molly

Whuppie's neck and her sisters'. But on his own daughters' necks he placed golden chains.

So when the giant had gone back down the ladder again, Molly sat up. She took the straw chain off of her own and her sisters' necks, and she took the golden chains off the giant's lassies. Then she exchanged them. After that, she lay down again and pretended to sleep. Oh, that Molly Whuppie was a clever girl!

In the middle of the night, the deep hind end of night when dangerous deeds get done and evil roams at will, the giant came back up the ladder to the loft. In the dark he felt at the neck of all the lassies, looking for the strands of straw. Then he picked up the girls—who were his own daughters—and carried them down the stairs, where he battered them with a club till they were all but dead. Then he lay down again to sleep, believing that he would have three earthly girls for breakfast.

As soon as Molly Whuppie heard him snoring, she woke her sisters up.

"Be quiet!" she warned them, and quiet they were. Then hand in hand in hand, they got out of the giant's house and ran and ran till they came to a grand house on the other side of the woods.

Now, that house was the king's own house. So Molly went right in and told him what had happened. Oh, that Molly Whuppie was a sturdy girl!

The king said, "Well, Molly, you have managed well. But you can manage better yet. Go back and steal the sword that hangs over the giant's bed, and I shall let your eldest sister marry my eldest son."

"I will surely try," said Molly Whuppie. Oh, that Molly Whuppie was a daring girl!

SO SHE WENT BACK, following her own trail, and slipped into the giant's house when the giant was out on one of his raids and his wife was bending over the cook pot. Then she quickly hid under his big bed and made not a sound.

The giant came home and ate up three sheep for supper. *Whooomp!* Just like that. And he didn't smell Molly because of the boiling cook pot. Then he went to bed and was fast asleep, his wife beside him.

Molly waited until they were both snoring, then she crept out from under the bed, stood carefully on the giant's bed, right above his pillow, and took down the sword. But just as she was about to get it free, the place on the bed where she was standing gave a rattle and she had to just grab the sword and run, for the giant awoke.

Out the door she went, with the giant right behind her. She ran and he ran, but she ran faster till she came to a bridge that was made of just one hair. Molly took a great deep breath and ran across it. She was so light, she skipped right over, but the giant did not dare go across.

He shook his great fist at her. "Ye near killed my girls, ye stole my sword!" he cried. "Woe unto ye, Molly Whuppie, if ye ever come here again."

But Molly only laughed and called back, "Twice yet I'll come to Spain!"

Then she took the sword to the king, and he had her eldest sister married to his eldest son that same day, though the feasting and dancing went on for seven.

Then the king said, "You have managed well, young Molly Whuppie. But you can do better yet. Go back and steal the purse that lies below the giant's pillow, and I will marry your second sister to my second son."

"I will surely try," said Molly Whuppie. Oh, that Molly Whuppie was a courageous girl!

SO SHE WENT BACK for the purse and hid in the giant's house without the giant or his wife knowing. And she bided her time till they slept again. Then she slipped her hand beneath the giant's pillow, and had just gotten

her hand on the purse, when the bed rattled again. So she had to just grab the purse and run, for the giant awoke.

Out the door she went, with the giant right behind her. She ran and he ran, but she ran faster till she came again to the bridge that was made of just one hair. Molly took a great deep breath and ran across it. She was so light, she skipped right over, but the giant did not dare go across.

He shook his great fist at her. "Ye near killed my girls, ye stole my sword, and now ye have my purse!" he cried. "Woe unto ye, Molly Whuppie, if ye ever come here again."

But Molly only laughed and called back, "Once yet I'll come to Spain!"

When she gave the purse to the king, he was good as his word, and her second sister was wed to his second son that very day. And the dancing and feasting went on for seven.

After it was done, the king said to Molly, "You have managed well, young Molly Whuppie. But you can do better yet. Go back and steal the finger ring that the giant wears, and I will give you my youngest son."

"I will surely try," said Molly Whuppie. Oh, that Molly Whuppie was an amazing girl!

So, back she went to the giant's house, and the giant ate and drank and went to bed with his wife. And once they were a-snoring, Molly went to the bed. With a touch as light as feather down, she picked up his hand. Then she pulled and pulled and pulled at the ring. But just as she got it off and placed it on her own hand as if it were a bracelet, the bed rattled and the giant awoke—and he gripped her by the hand.

"I have ye now, Molly Whuppie. Ye near killed my girls and stole my sword and purse. But ye shall not go unpunished. I would do as much to ye as ye have done to me. Now, what would ye do to me?"

Molly spoke up at once. "I would put you in a sack. I'd put the cat inside with you and the dog beside the cat, that they could gnaw on your bones. I'd add a needle to prick you, thread to tie you, shears to cut you.

Then I'd hang that sack up on the wall. And then I'd go into the wood to choose the biggest stick I could find. A tree trunk would do. And home I'd come to bang that sack with the stick till you were dead as dead."

"Well, Molly, ye have said it well. I will do just that to ye." So he got the sack and put Molly in it, with his ugly cat and the dog beside her. Then he popped in the needle and thread and shears. He hung the sack on the wall, told his wife to watch it carefully, and then off he went to the wood.

"Oh, do you see what I see?" sang out Molly Whuppie from the sack.

"Oh, what do ye see?" asked the giant's wife.

"The most beautiful thing in the world," said Molly Whuppie.

"Let me see, too!" cried the giant's wife.

"You'd have to be here with me," said Molly.

"I can't take the sack down," said the giant's wife.

"Then I shall take you up," said Molly. She took out the shears, cut a hole in the sack just big enough for herself, and jumped out, carrying the needle and thread. She boosted the giant's wife into the sack and quickly sewed up the hole.

"I don't see a thing," said the giant's wife.

"Keep looking!" cried Molly. Then she hid herself behind the door, for just then, in came the giant carrying a great tree.

He took down the sack and began to batter it.

His wife cried out, "Stop! Stop, ye old fool! It's me! It's me!" But the dog barked so and the cat mewed so, the giant could not hear her.

Molly Whuppie ran out the door, and just then the giant saw her. He was so mad, he bit down on his knuckle and stopped beating the sack. Then he ran out after her.

Molly ran and he ran, but she ran faster till she came to the bridge of one hair. She was so light, she just skipped over, but the giant did not dare go across.

He shook his big fist at her. "Ye near killed my girls, ye stole my sword and purse and ring, and now ye have had me beat my wife!" he cried. "Woe unto ye, Molly Whuppie, if ye ever come here again."

But Molly only laughed. "Never more will I come to Spain!" she told him.

Then she took the ring to the king, and she married the king's youngest son that very day. And there was feasting and dancing for a month.

Molly and the youngest son ruled in the kingdom ever after. And she never saw the giant again. Lucky for him. That Molly Whuppie was a hero!

An Open Letter to Nana

YOU SAID WE NEEDED this book, and we do. But not for the reasons you think. We already know that girls have power, that we can be heroes, too. We already take kendo and judo and have black belts in karate. We are already on school wrestling teams and soccer teams and can outrun the boys in track. And we can do it all with polished nails, if we like.

Hi, Xena!

Hi, Diana of the Hunt!

Hi, Atalanta!

But we need this book to remind ourselves that girl heroes have always been around, hidden away—as you say—in the back storeroom of folklore.

And we need this book because these great stories need a shaking out every so often, like some old camp blanket that's been packed away all year.

And boys need to read it, too. Because while *we* know girls can be heroes, the boys need to know it even more.

Your loving daughter and granddaughters

Notes on the Stories

An Open Letter to My Daughters and Granddaughters

I learned about many of the fighting women mentioned in this introduction in a marvelous chock-full book called *Women Warriors: A History* by David E. Jones (Brassey's, Inc., 1997). But I already knew about the women pirates. The very first book I ever wrote was *Pirates in Petticoats* (David McKay, 1963), a nonfiction book about women pirates for which I did a year's worth of research.

"Atalanta the Huntress"

The story of Atalanta begins like many of the great hero tales and stories about feral children. A child is set out on a hillside, is nursed by an animal, and grows up with amazing powers. In this instance she becomes a great huntress and runner.

I have taken the actual story of the Calydonian hunt from the poet Ovid's *Metamorphoses*, book 8, lines 273–532, and the story of Atalanta's race from there (book 10, lines 560–707) and numerous other sources as well.

These are really two separate stories and may actually be about two different girls called Atalanta, one a legend from Arcadia and the other from Boeotia.

The spelling of Melanion's name is also given as Milanion. In Ovid's telling he is called Hippomenes, and Aphrodite is, of course, called Venus.

Though I have ended the story happily ever after, it usually goes on as follows: Traveling home from a long trip, Atalanta and her husband come upon a hidden temple in the forest. The temple belongs to Zeus, to Rhea, to Aphrodite—the stories vary. They lie down to sleep. Overcome by passion the couple desecrate the temple by making love there. The god (Zeus, Rhea, Aphrodite, whoever) is furious and turns them into great lions with—as Ovid puts it—"tails sweeping the sandy ground." This is a terrible punishment, even more terrible to the ancients, who believed that lions only mated with leopards. But I prefer to leave our hero and her new husband with many happy years ahead. Peace, Artemis.

"Nana Miriam"

Nana Miriam is a culture hero of the Songhai people. And as with many culture heroes, her power is more magical than physical, though what is particularly interesting about her is that she is quite strong as well.

This story can be found in Steven H. Gale's *West African Folktales.* I have added both cultural information (names of Niger River fish and Niger proverbs) and storytelling bits (like the descriptions of the dogs). And I have made more distinct the fact that the cliff rock—and not a human being—actually kills the unkillable monster, a theme that is only hinted at in the Gale version of the tale.

The transformational powers of a monster/ogre/devil are quite common in stories from around the world. What makes this one different—and very African—is that the monster's main shape is that of a hippopotamus!

"Fitcher's Bird"

The tale of Fitcher's bird is in a long tradition of demon-lover stories. It comes from the Grimms' collection of folktales. Known as Mr. Fox in England, Reynadine in other parts of the British Isles, Bluebeard in the Perrault collection, Silver Nose in Italy (see the Italo Calvino *Italian Folktales* collection), Fitcher's bird can be found throughout Europe in innumerable versions. There are American adaptations of Mr. Fox as well. The story always involves a murderous king or sorcerer or merchant or troll—or the devil himself. This evil character marries (or hires) a succession of sisters, all of whom are warned about a certain door into a forbidden room.

Interesting to note, there is a custom stemming from the nineteenth century to illustrate the wicked sorcerer as an "Oriental"—the consummate outsider to Europeans and Americans.

This story is so well known, it is called tale type 311 in Stith Thompson's great database of story types, which folklorists use. But its various parts have their own motif numbers as well, for example: "forbidden chamber," C611, and "forbidden door," C611.1.

Sometimes the sisters are saved by their brothers. More often the youngest sister saves them all. Usually she is clever—as in this story, "Fitcher's Bird." Occasionally—as in a Basque version of the story—she actually dispatches the villain with a saber herself! But as Marina Warner says in her fascinating book *From the Beast to the Blonde*, "the narrative concentrates on [the girl's] act of disobedience, not on [the sorcerer's] mass murders." In many versions there is a subtitle to the story: "The Effect of Female Curiosity" or "The Fatal Effects of Curiosity," and similar tags. And in the Mr. Fox variant, the very walls of his house have the following legend painted on them: "Be bold, be bold, but not too bold." But in fact, if the one girl were not bold and clever—as is Erna in this story—all would be lost.

I have used the basic outline of the Grimms' story, but I have told the story in my own way—adding such things as the girl's names, the dialogue, the way the devil walks, and the use of the egg in the end (the Grimms' story says she uses a "death's head")—to make the story fresh again.

"The Girl and the Puma"

This story is a legend rather than a folktale—that is, it is a magic story set in a real place. Buenos Aires was settled first in 1536, but inadequate food supplies and poor treatment of the local Indians were to be the settlement's undoing. The siege and the battles with the local *indios* mentioned in the story are real. In 1541 the few remaining settlers of Buenos Aires moved to Asunción. Buenos Aires was not to be resettled for another forty years. In Uruguay there *is* a city called Maldonado, which is supposedly named after the brave and kind señorita. Although in this telling I make the villain Captain Francisco Ruiz Galán, in other tellings his part is taken by a certain Captain Alvarado.

Farming among the Indians was confined to the lower slopes of the Andes and the borders of the Río de la Plata.

The rest of the story is pure folktale, some influenced by Spanish lore and some—no doubt—by Indian tellings.

I found this story both in *The King of the Mountains: A Treasury of Latin American Folk Stories*, collected by Moritz A. Jagendorf and R. S. Boggs, and through my Argentine friends Sibela Martin and her son, Chris Pedregal Martin. Sibela translated it for me from the famous *Argentina manuscripta*, the account by Ruy Díaz de Guzmán, a nephew of Alvar Nuñez Cabeza de Vaca. Ruy Diáz de Guzmán was born in Asunción between 1554 and 1560, and died in that city in 1629. Between 1610 and 1614 he wrote the report, which went unpublished for two hundred years. Doubtless related to the founders of the fort, he was writing about events that took place from around 1536 to 1540.

Isabel de Guevara was one of the women actually in the fort, and she wrote to Queen Juana of Spain:

Very High and Mighty Lady: to this province of the La Plata river, with its first governor, don Pedro de Mendoza, came certain women, between them my fate has determined that I am one of them. And as the Armada arrived to the port of Buenos Ayres with thousand five hundred men and they lacked supplies, hunger was so terrible that it cannot be compared to the one of Jerusalem, there is none that can be compared to it. The men became so weak that all the work was done by the poor women, they washed their clothes, they healed them, they prepared meals with what little they had, they cleaned them, they were the sentinels, they kept the fires, they armed the crossbows when sometimes the Indians came to make war . . . they gave the alarm out in the country sometimes, giving orders and ordering to the soldiers, because in that time, as the women survive with little food, we weren't as weak as men. Her Majesty will have to believe it that without so much the care of the women, all would have been finished, and if it wouldn't be because of the honour of those men I would write much more and would call them as witnesses.

The story of Señorita Maldonada and the puma is a popular folk legend of the area, but it is based on the real and terrible founding of Buenos Aires. My telling combines elements from both story lines, but the dialogue, descriptions, and wordings are my own.

"Li Chi Slays the Serpent"

The story in a much plainer telling—without dialogue or ornamentation—can be found in *Chinese Fairy Tales and Fantasies,* translated and edited by Moss Roberts. The story is from the Chin dynasty of China.

There are hundreds of stories in China in which snakes or serpents figure, most often as dangers, but occasionally—as in the story called "The Tale of Nung-kua-ma" (see Wolfram Eberhard's *Folktales of China*), in which a snake catcher uses poisonous snakes to kill a monster—they are helpful creatures. However, Chinese snakes must never be mistaken for dragons. In Western tales snakes and dragons are often interchangeable. But in China the dragons are of a higher nature, elemental creatures—gods of the rains and floods.

The sacrifice of young maidens to a serpent-monster is certainly a popular motif in European folk stories. In the most popular European version (tale type 300) there are recognizable parallels to Li Chi's story: A dragon lives in the mountains. It devours sacrificial maidens on a regular basis else—it warns—it will lay waste to the countryside. A princess is the next chosen one. (From then on the Chinese story is quite different.) A young man of little stature or worth volunteers, with his dog, to slay the creature, and his reward is marriage to the princess, and half the kingdom. He does slay the monster, and at this point—when the Chinese story effectively ends—the European story takes off in an entirely new direction.

"Brave Woman Counts Coup"

This story was first recorded by folklorist Richard Erdoes at the White River Rosebud Indian Reservation in South Dakota, 1967. The teller was Jenny Leading Cloud. That version can be found in *American Indian Myths and Legends,* selected and edited by Richard Erdoes and Alfonso Ortiz. It is clear from that telling, Jenny Leading Cloud considered this not a folktale but a true story.

Even as a true story it has many elements of a folktale—or a legend, which is a traveling story that gets set in a real time and place but is problematical as to its authenticity.

"Pretty Penny"

Much-condensed variations of this story can be found in Vance Randolph's *The Devil's Pretty Daughter* and in "The Maid of Rygate," a British ballad sung also in America that goes back as far as 1769, when it appeared in *Logan's Pedlar's Pack,* number 133. Both are based on the more widely known song "The Crafty Farmer," Child ballad number 283, in which a farmer throws his old saddlebag over the hedge to tempt the thief, then rides off on the robber's own horse. The Randolph version and "The Maid of Rygate," like mine, make the hero a girl.

My plot is somewhat similar to that of the prose story, but I've added a particular voice, named the characters, given them dialogue, described the girl (she is only called "a big stout girl about sixteen years old" in Randolph's version), and so forth. Because Penny first fights the road agent and then fools him, I think of her as a double hero.

"Burd Janet"

This story is most often called "Tam Lin," but as this book is about strong young women—which Janet surely is—I have renamed the story for her.

The story comes from the popular Scottish border ballad—Child ballad number 35—which was first mentioned in a ballad book from 1549 as "The Tayl of the song Tamlene." It has been told in story form for at least the past hundred years, most popularly by Joseph Jacobs. The telling in *Not One Damsel in Distress* is based on my own picture-book telling, *Tam Lin,* with glorious pictures by Charles Mikolaycak. There are also short story versions (one by Robin McKinley is especially wonderful) and three novels, which all use the ballad, that are particular favorites of mine: *Tam Lin* by Pamela Dean, *Fire and Hemlock* by Diana Wynne Jones, and *The Perilous Gard* by Elizabeth Marie Pope.

Most of the details in this telling come from the ballad, though certainly the idea of shape changing goes even further back than that in world folklore—to Greece even before Homer. And some of the details in this telling also come from Scottish folk wisdom (the bit about the bones of the herring, for example).

There is a plain on the river Yarrow, near Selkirk, called Carterhaugh, as well as a great old farmhouse (not a castle). I have been there.

"Mizilca"

This Romanian story from an old ballad can be found in a shorter version in *Clever Gretchen and Other Forgotten Folktales*, in which it is retold by Alison Lurie, and in a longer and more Victorian version as "The Girl Who Pretended to Be a Boy" in Andrew Lang's *The Violet Fairy Book*. The ballad itself—in a version that includes a magic talking horse—can be read in Erich Seeman's *European Folk Ballads*.

This is a folk story that is popular throughout Europe and is directly related to the German story "The Twelve Huntsmen," as well as to the Arabic story "The Story of the King, Hamed bin Bathara" and to the tale of the "Fearless Girl" (see C. G. Campbell's *From Town and Tribe*), which can be found in Oman and Iraq. It is also quite close to the Sudanese story "Yousif Al-Saffani," found in Ahmed Al-Shahi and F. C. T. Moore's *Wisdom of the Nile* collection. I have borrowed one of the gender tests—the peas underfoot—from the German tale and added it to the story to make three (that magic number) tests. In "The Twelve Huntsmen" the other tests include displaying spinning wheels in the hall "because women always look at spinning wheels with eager interest" and shooting bows "because a woman cannot shoot an arrow as a man can." "The Twelve Huntsmen" can be found in both *The Green Fairy Book* by Andrew Lang and *The Maid of the North: Feminist Folk Tales from Around the World* by Ethel Johnston Phelps. In the Arabic story the tests are silks and swords, a pepper-and-cloves meal, whipping a child, and bathing in the sea. In the Sudanese story the tests are dates with stones in them, hunting and catching something, climbing a tree to the top (this is a menstrual-cycle trial), swords and dresses at the market, a massage, and bathing in the river. In each case the girl outwits the sultan/king.

Young women who disguise themselves as men and go off to battle are popular not only in folk stories but in legends and history as well. There are instances of disguised American women doing battle in both the Civil and Revolutionary Wars; British women with shorn hair and wearing pants were recorded as having served aboard ship, et cetera. Perhaps the most famous of these disguised soldiers were

Deborah Samson, who fought in the American Revolution, and Ann Bonney and Mary Reade, who were pirates under Captain "Calico" Jack Rackham.

"The Pirate Princess"

I based my telling on Howard Schwartz's, which he got from the Hebrew *Sippure Maasiyot* by Rabbi Nachman of Bratslav, edited by Rabbi Nathan Sternhartz of Nemirov (Warsaw, 1881). Schwartz's version can be found in *Elijah's Violin & Other Jewish Fairy Tales*, a wonderful collection of retold tales. While I followed Schwartz's plotline fairly closely, I added dialogue and bits of special action.

Rabbi Nachman lived in Bratslav, Poland, in the nineteenth century. He was the great-grandson of the famous Hassidic rabbi, storyteller, and wonder worker the Ba'al Shem Tov, who began the Hassidic tradition in Jewish life two hundred years ago. The Hassids are an ecstatic sect, worshiping in dance and song as well as study. In less than three generations, the Hassids numbered more than half of the Jews in Eastern Europe. They had their own rabbis, or "exalted saints," who governed them. It was said by Meyer Levin in *Classic Hassidic Tales* that in Rabbi Nachman the "Hassidic legend had its fulfillment and completion." That is, while Rabbi Nachman drew heavily on folk sources, he spun out stories that were his own tellings. They were folk compilations, told not just to entertain but to enlighten, elucidate, and to make wise the listeners.

This story is about the working out of fate for two promised lovers, which was more an Eastern than a Western concept, and one which the Hassids embraced. It is episodic, meaning each of the adventures is a little story itself, but the entire thing wraps around and fits together, dovetailed, in the end.

"The Samurai Maiden"

I first discovered this story in Kathleen Ragan's *Fearless Girls, Wise Women, and Beloved Sisters*, though in her notes she says it comes from *Folk and Fairy Tales of Far-off Lands*, edited by Eric and Nancy Protter. In both instances the story is called "The Tale of the Oki Islands." It bears a strong relationship to the Chinese story "Li Chi Slays the Dragon," for in each the brave young maiden hero takes the place of a girl who is to be sacrificed to an evil serpent-god.

The sacrifice of young maidens to a serpent-monster (tale type 300) is a popular motif in European folk stories. That this story takes place underwater rather than in the mountain fasts of most European tales is one of the things that is so special about it. Tokoyo's previous experience as a Japanese pearl diver is a unique touch.

I have followed the outline of the story but added both dialogue and Tokoyo's old nurse to the tale.

"Bradamante"

The story of Bradamante is not one story but a series of legendary adventures about a knight of the great king Charlemagne, whose legends were to France what Arthur's were to Britain, except that Charlemagne himself was much more of a historical figure. Charlemagne (or Charles the Great) came to the throne in A.D. 768.

According to Thomas Bulfinch, whose original *Legends of Charlemagne* was completed and first published in 1863:

> There is, however, a pretended history, which was for a long time admitted as authentic, and attributed to Turpin, Archbishop of Rheims, a real personage at the time of Charlemagne.... It is now unhesitatingly considered as a collection of popular traditions, produced by some credulous and unscrupulous monk.

Turpin's "account," as well as the more fabulous and legendary materials that have accumulated around Charlemagne's name, have led to many wonderful stories. The most famous of these is *The Song of Roland*.

I have followed the outline of Bulfinch's telling, for the most part, but added much dialogue while leaving out considerable bowing and scraping. The rescue-from-the-castle story of Bradamante and her true love, Ruggiero, actually ends badly as one of the hippogriffs runs off with him, depositing him on an island far away. It is many more adventures before they come together again. But for the purposes of this retelling, we can skip ahead to the happy-ever-after.

"Molly Whuppie"

This story made its way from the folk consciousness into Joseph Jacobs's collection *English Fairy Tales*. "Molly Whuppie" remains the single most popular strong-female story in the British Isles. It is unclear whether it is English or Scottish. The giant, at least, seems somewhat Scottish, calling his daughters "lassies."

The story is related both to "Jack and the Beanstalk" and (in its opening at least) to "Hansel and Gretel," but it has its own tale type, number 327, "the children and the ogre," in which the hero fools the very wicked—and extremely stupid—giant. In fact, the hero is usually a boy, and only in the Molly Whuppie variant is the lead role taken unequivocally by a girl. In *"Le Petit Poucet,"* the French version (tale type 327B), the exchange made by the hero to fool the giant is of hats, not straw ropes and golden chains. So popular is this story, it exists throughout Europe and it even found its way—through French traders—to Indian tribes in British Columbia.

The giant's verse is, of course, familiar. Or perhaps all British giants recite variations of the same verse: "Fe-fi-fo-fum . . ."

The section of the story in which the hero is put in the sack is a popular motif and can be found in different European tales—especially in Norway and the Baltic states (tale type 327C, "the hero escapes from the sack by substituting some animal or object"). There are some African American stories and some Native American stories that also use this same trick, though Stith Thompson believes this is more likely to have been invented by them than borrowed, as it is such a simple substitution.

There are some scholars who feel that the "bridge of one hair" comes out of Arabic storytelling, as there is a bridge as fine as a single hair over which Muslims pass on their way into heaven. Joseph Campbell cites the Scottish variant of the story, *"Maol a Chilobain,"* because in it the female hero plucks a hair of her own and it turns into a bridge.

There is a popular American version of the Molly Whuppie variant called "Mutsmeg," which can be found in Richard Chase's *Grandfather Tales,* and a version in which it is a boy servant—Nippy—who is the hero, in "Nippy and the Giants," found in the American South.

Bibliography

"Atalanta the Huntress"

d'Aulaire, Ingri, and Edgar Parin. *Ingri and Edgar Parin d'Aulaire's Book of Greek Myths.* Garden City, New York: Doubleday & Company, Inc., 1962.

Godolphin, Francis Richard Borroum, ed. *Great Classical Myths.* New York: The Modern Library/Random House, 1964.

Grimal, Pierre. *The Dictionary of Classical Mythology.* Translated by A. R. Maxwell-Hyslop. Oxford: Blackwell Publishers, Inc., 1985.

Schwab, Gustav. *Gods and Heroes: Myths and Epics of Ancient Greece.* New York: Pantheon, 1974.

Tripp, Edward. *The Meridian Handbook of Classical Mythology.* New York: New American Library, 1970.

"Nana Miriam"

Encyclopaedia Britannica, s.v. "Niger." 1967.

Gale, Steven H. *West African Folktales.* Lincolnwood, Illinois: NTC Publishing Group, 1995.

Leslau, Charlotte and Wolf, comps. *African Proverbs.* Mount Vernon, New York: Peter Pauper Press, 1982.

Thompson, Stith. *The Folktale.* Berkeley, California: University of California Press, 1977.

"Fitcher's Bird"

Calvino, Italo. *Italian Folktales.* Translated by George Martin. New York: Pantheon Books, 1980.

Grimms' Fairy Tales. London: Adam & Charles Black, 1911.

Warner, Marina. *From the Beast to the Blonde: On Fairy Tales and Their Tellers.* New York: Farrar, Straus and Giroux, 1995.

Zipes, Jack, trans. *The Complete Fairy Tales of the Brothers Grimm.* New York: Bantam Books, 1987.

"The Girl and the Puma"

de Guevara, Isabel. Letter to Queen Juana of Spain. Translated for the author by Sibela Martin.

de Guzmán, Ruy Díaz. *Argentina manuscripta.* Translated for the author by Sibela Martin.

Encyclopaedia Britannica, s.v. "Argentina." 1967.

Jagendorf, Moritz A., and R. S. Boggs. *The King of the Mountains: A Treasury of Latin American Folk Stories.* New York: Vanguard Press, 1960.

"Li Chi Slays the Serpent"

Eberhard, Wolfram. *Folktales of China.* Chicago: University of Chicago Press, 1965.

Roberts, Moss, trans. and ed. *Chinese Fairy Tales and Fantasies.* New York: Pantheon Books, 1979.

Thompson, Stith. *The Folktale.* Berkeley, California: University of California Press, 1977.

"Brave Woman Counts Coup"

Brown, Dee Alexander. *Tepee Tales of the American Indian.* New York: Holt, Rinehart, and Winston, 1979.

Erdoes, Richard, and Alfonso Ortiz, eds. *American Indian Myths and Legends.* New York: Pantheon Books, 1984.

"Pretty Penny"

Child, Francis James, editor. *The English and Scottish Popular Ballads*, vol. 5. Boston: Houghton Mifflin Company, 1898.

Flanders, Helen Hartness. *Ancient Ballads Traditionally Sung in New England.* Philadelphia: University of Pennsylvania Press, 1960.

Randolph, Vance. *The Devil's Pretty Daughter.* New York: Columbia University Press, 1955.

Stemple, F. J., my father-in-law, who lived more than sixty years in Webster Springs, West Virginia, and told stories in just the manner I used for this story.

"Burd Janet"

Child, Francis James, editor. *The English and Scottish Popular Ballads,* vol. 1. New York: Dover Publications, 1965.

Douglas, Ronald Macdonald, comp. *The Scots Book of Lore and Folklore.* New York: E. P. Dutton & Company.

Yolen, Jane. *Tam Lin.* San Diego, California: Harcourt Brace & Company, 1990.

"Mizilca"

Lang, Andrew, ed. *The Green Fairy Book.* New York: Dover Publications, Inc., 1965.
———. *The Violet Fairy Book.* New York: Dover Publications, Inc., 1967.

Lurie, Alison. *Clever Gretchen and Other Forgotten Folktales.* New York: Thomas Y. Crowell, 1980.

Phelps, Ethel Johnston. *The Maid of the North: Feminist Folk Tales from Around the World.* New York: Holt, Rinehart, and Winston, 1981.

Seeman, Erich, Dag Stromback, and Bengt R. Jonsson. *European Folk Ballads,* vol. 2. Copenhagen: Rosenkilde and Bagger, 1967.

Thompson, Stith. *The Folktale.* Berkeley, California: University of California Press, 1977.

"The Pirate Princess"

Levin, Meyer. *Classic Hassidic Tales.* New York: Dorset Press, 1959.

Schwartz, Howard. *Elijah's Violin & Other Jewish Fairy Tales.* New York: Harper & Row, 1983.

"The Samurai Maiden"

Protter, Eric and Nancy, eds. *Folk and Fairy Tales of Far-off Lands.* Translated by Robert Egan. New York: Duell, Sloane and Pearce, 1965.

Ragan, Kathleen, ed. *Fearless Girls, Wise Women, and Beloved Sisters.* New York: W. W. Norton & Company, 1998.

Thompson, Stith. *The Folktale.* Berkeley, California: University of California Press, 1977.

"Bradamante"

Bulfinch, Thomas. *Bulfinch's Mythology: The Age of Chivalry and Legends of Charlemagne.* New York: Meridian Books, 1995.
———. *Bulfinch's Mythology.* Abridged by Edmund Fuller. New York: Dell, 1975.

"Molly Whuppie"

Burrison, John A., ed. *Storytellers: Folktales & Legends from the South.* Athens, Georgia: University of Georgia Press, 1991.

Clarkson, Atelia, and Gilbert B. Cross, eds. *World Folktales.* New York: Charles Scribner's Sons, 1980.

Cole, Joanna, comp. *Best-Loved Folktales of the World.* Garden City, New York: Doubleday, 1983.

Lurie, Alison. *Clever Gretchen and Other Forgotten Folktales.* New York: Thomas Y. Crowell, 1980.

Thompson, Stith. *The Folktale.* Berkeley, California: University of California Press, 1977.